The Cardboard House

The Cardboard House

Martín Adán

Translated and with an introduction by Katherine Silver
Afterword translated by Katherine Silver and Rick London

A NEW DIRECTIONS PAPERBOOK

Translation copyright © 2012 by Katherine Silver
Introduction copyright © 1990, 2012 by Katherine Silver
Afterword translation copyright © 2012 by Katherine Silver and Rick London

Published originally in Peru as *La casa de carton* in 1928.

Manufactured in the United States of America
Published simultaneously in Canada by Penguin Books Canada, Ltd.
New Directions Books are printed on acid-free paper.
First published as a New Directions Paperbook (ND1235) in 2012.

Library of Congress Cataloging-in-Publication Data
Adán, Martín, 1908–1985.
[Casa de cartón. English]
The cardboard house / Martin Adan ; translated and with an introduction by
    Katherine Silver ; with an afterword, translated by Katherine Silver and Rick
    London.
p. cm.
ISBN 978-0-8112-1959-4 (acid-free paper)
I. Silver, Katherine. II. London, Rick. III. Title.
PQ8497.F83C313 2012
863—dc23

                            2012014670

New Directions Books are published for James Laughlin
by New Directions Publishing Corporation,
80 Eighth Avenue, New York 10011

to José María Eguren

Contents

Translator's Preface

THE CLIFFS OVERLOOKING THE PACIFIC OCEAN ARE only a ten-minute bus ride away from the dirty, crowded, ash-colored streets of downtown Lima. *Beyond the city: the clear tender chasm of the sea.* Walking south on the esplanade that winds along the edge of these cliffs, you soon reach *the last stretch on the way to Chorrillos, zigzagging, seascape in relief, carved with a knife, a sailor's toy.* Along the way, you are flanked on your left by the sea that *is never glaucous, but instead has pale, colorless zones, lined with the tracks of ducks, full of minute coasts and feeble backgrounds.* Scattered here and there along Barranco's esplanade are *ancient gardens of fragile roses and dirty and dwarfed palm trees … with one hour of quietude: six o'clock in the afternoon.*

Continuing in the same direction, you happen upon the plaza of Barranco: there is a pond, trees with bulbous trunks and thorns and bright pink flowers, and *a plaster of Paris Eros with a terrible parrot perched on its head.* The avenues leading out from the plaza are lined with jacaranda trees that *produce many purple flowers … a solemn, old-fashioned, confidential, expressive, gaudy, mindful, family* tree. A newspaper vendor stands on one corner, and his *Crónica and Comercio* newspapers are blown about until the cart threatens to roll backwards. On another street corner stands *a pretty native woman with her hard, shiny, damp head of hair—a mud carving*—selling her single cigarettes and chewing gum.

This is the setting—geographically—of *The Cardboard House*. To find it in time, we must turn back to the first few decades of the twentieth century when Martín Adán, né Rafael de la Fuente Benavides, spent his summer vacations with his family in what was a slightly seedy but still exclusive seaside resort. When Adán began composing *The Cardboard House* at the age of eighteen, Barranco for him was also fragments of memory, imagination, sensations, nostalgic yearnings. The resort, as he had known it—and his place in it—had ceased to exist. His family, aristocratic but in full economic decadence, had sold their Barranco chalet some years earlier to pay off debts.

Biographical information is sparse and anecdotal. Rafael de la Fuente was born in Lima in 1908. By the time he was a young adult, he had lost every member of his immediate family: his younger brother died when they were children; his father, his mother, and finally the aunt and uncle under whose care he had been placed followed soon thereafter. He attended the German High School, where many of his classmates and teachers were or would become leading figures in Peru's artistic and intellectual life of the twentieth century.

When *The Cardboard House* appeared in 1928, it was received with high critical acclaim, published within the warm embrace of a prologue by Luis Alberto Sánchez and an afterword by José Carlos Maríategui. Adán was hailed as a great innovator of Peruvian literature and the most promising young writer of his generation. For several years he moved in Lima's literary circles and marginally participated in the political and cultural debates that raged at that time.

Then, the traces of his life fade into an alcoholic haze. There are anecdotes about the coffee houses he visited, the odd scraps of napkin on which he wrote his poems, his increasing isolation, and the long periods of internment in hospitals and clinics of various kinds. He died in 1985, his final years spent shunning all public attention and only allowing visits from his editor, Juan Mejía Baca, and a few close friends. During one of the few interviews he ever granted—and only after the interviewer had spent years soliciting a meeting, one that Adán cut short after a few questions—he said he wrote *The Cardboard House* to practice the rules his grammar professor, Emilio Huidobro, had given him.

Perhaps the notebook that housed his words was cardboard like those in Miss Muler's classroom.

The Cardboard House is the only prose text Martín Adán ever completed. Some six or seven volumes of poetry were published during his lifetime and this due largely to the painstaking and devoted labor of Mejía Baca, who collected the bits and pieces of paper Adán left strewn along his path. He is now considered to be one of the greatest Latin American poets of all time.

I am not wholly convinced of my own humanity; I do not wish to be like others. I do not want to be happy with permission of the police.

The world is insufficient for me.

The Cardboard House is composed of a series of fragments or scenes. Each fragment, and even each image within each fragment, is a world unto itself, vibrating through Adán's power of evocation. Most critics have given up looking for any thematic or narrative development, and only the narrator and Ramón—

his friend, alter ego, and rival—could possibly qualify as characters. Adán borrows—from Proust, from Joyce, from Góngora—but he laughs at himself for doing so, as he laughs at his nation for that *native and premature desire that Europe will make of us men.* He makes no bones about who he is: a provincial boy in a semicolonial world who experiences the modern world as it is exported to him. "Gringos" appear right next to "Indians." They look, smell, talk, and act differently. *This one was an Englishman who fished with a rod ... A poet? Nothing of the sort: a travel agent from Dawson and Brothers Ltd.... Or Miss Annie Doll ... Synthetic milk, canned meat, hard liquor ... a red, long, sinewy, mobile thing that carries a Kodak over its shoulder and asks questions that are wise, useless, and nonsensical.*

This translation of *The Cardboard House* was first published in 1990 by Graywolf Press. It has been my good fortune, and delight, to review my younger efforts and make significant though not extensive changes for this edition. In some cases, I have corrected outright errors (and would like to thank Dr. Grace Aaron for pointing out a few), caused by inadvertency or mistaken interpretations; in others, I found what I think now to be a more elegant and truer way to render Adán's Spanish into English while retaining, hopefully even more closely, the sense and sound of the original. Coming back to this text twenty years later, I find this small, unique gem from the seacoast of the south shimmering even more brightly, but I now perceive more fully the swirls of darkness that would so overwhelm the poet's life.

Included in this edition is a fragment that appeared in a literary magazine, *Amauta,* in 1927, and then excluded from the whole when it was published the following year.

Also included is "Written Blindly," translated in collaboration with Rick London. It is another genre-bending piece written more than thirty years after *The Cardboard House*. Epistle, poem, autobiographical note: its inclusion here draws an evocative poetic trajectory from the beginning to somewhere in the middle, a trajectory strewn with scribbled scraps: words. As Adán asks: *What is the Word / but a vain and varied shout?*

KATHERINE SILVER

The Cardboard House

WINTER IN BARRANCO HAS ALREADY BEGUN — A peculiar, daft, and fragile winter that might just cleave the sky and let a tip of summer peek through. The mist of this small winter, affairs of the soul, puffs of sea breeze, drizzles of a boat trip from one pier to another, the sonorous flutter of rushing lay-sisters, opaque sounds of Mass, winter newly arrived ... Now, off to school with cold hands. Breakfast is a warm ball in the stomach, the hardness of the dining room chair on the buttocks, and the solemn desire in the entire body not to go to school. The frond of a palm tree hovers over a house: flabellate, gently somber, pure, pink, glistening. And now you whistle with the streetcar, boy with closed eyes. You do not understand how one can possibly go to school so early in the morning, especially when there are esplanades and the sea below. But as you walk down the street that traverses almost the entire city, you smell the perfume of distant vegetables in nearby gardens. You think of the lush, wet fields, almost urban behind you, limitless in front of you, between the ash and elder trees, toward the bluish sierra. Barely the outline of the first foothills, the mountains' eyebrow ... And now you pass through the fields surrounded by muffled beehive sounds of fleeting friction over rails and a flourish of

3

athletic though urban gymnastics. Now the sun grinds to golden a mountain peak and an ancient burial mound, a yellow knoll like the sun itself. And you do not want it to be summer, but rather winter vacation, tiny and weak, with no school and no heat.

BEYOND THE FIELDS: THE SIERRA; BEFORE THE FIELDS: a creek lined with alder trees and women washing clothes and children, all the same color of indifferent dirt. It is two o'clock in the afternoon. The sun struggles to free its rays from the branches into which it has fallen captive. The sun—a rare, hard, golden, lanky coleopteran. Father Parish Priest doffs his shovel hat, tilts his head; eleven reflections off a tall silk hat, a top hat— those eleven reflections converge overhead in a round, convex light. Beyond the city: the clear, tender chasm of the sea. The sea can be seen from above, at the risk of slipping down the slope. The cliffs have wrinkles and spotless smooth patches and are livid and jaundiced on their geological, academic foreheads. There, in miniature, are the four ages of the world, the four dimensions of all things, the four cardinal points, everything, everything. One old man … Two old men … Three old men … Three Pierolistas. Three hours of sunshine must be wrested from the night. Oversized garments hang loosely off the body. The smooth cloth is squared, trihedral, falls, grows taut—the cloth: empty within. Bones creak in time with timed gestures, with the rhythmic stretching of hands to the sky of the horizon—the plane that intersects that of the sea to form angle X, last chapter of beginning geometry (first semester)—the sky where Pierola most likely is. The old men's whiskers slice the sea breeze into fine strips like expensive jelly and infuse it with the scent of guava trees, tobacco from Tumbes, herb-scented handkerchiefs, local concoctions for coughs. A six-colored flag, wafted gently by a high wind not felt from below, suggests the flanks of a Spanish dancer. The Consulate General of Tomesia—a country created by Giraudoux out of a Hungarian plain, two Lima millionaires, several English trees, and the tone of an embroidered Chinese sky. Tomesia: never far from its Consulate General. The ice cream vendor's cart goes past an old nag dangling its rough, blanched tongue. The poor beast would love to lick the ices in the hidden bucket; elegant and opaque lucuma-flavored ices, just barely chilled; ice creams, ample and pretty like a youthful portrait of Mother sitting beside Father; pineapple-flavored ices that go with red carnations; light and unfamiliar orange-flavored ices. How this cart does sound! The poor thing tears its soul out on the stones. Yet it would not alter its course for anything in the world—its straight course past the walls of the dead-end street, straight into imbecility. O little cart, cross over this lawn kept smooth for you by the water of the fountain. Between things there exist bonds of mutual aid hampered by man. The rumble of the cart's wheels on the paving stones gladdens the sad waters of the fountain. The mestizo with cheeks the color of blood-soaked earth, his nose sprinkled with tiny, round drops of sweat—the mestizo cart driver does not allow the cart to roll over the lawn of that meager garden. The old men comment: "It's cold." "Yesterday?" "A beautiful day!" "Whatever you say, Menganez ..."

IN THE MORNING, ON THE SHARP EDGE OF DAWN, from the casement windows of the towers and in the awkward flight of frightened birds and the soggy bells, the old lay-sisters descend through the fog to their witches' Sabbath of trees and poles. Black bulks sway to and fro, an infinity of arms, clawed hands, mumbled watchwords ... And the city is an oleograph we contemplate, sunken under water: the waves carry things away and alter the orientation of the planes. Lay-sisters who smell of sun and dew; of the dampness of towels left behind bathtubs; of elixirs, eyewash, the devil, sponges; that dry, hollow smell of a soapy, worn, discolored pumice stone ... Lay-sisters who smell of dirty clothes, stars, cat fur, lamp oil, sperm ... Lay-sisters who smell of weeds, darkness, the litany, flowers for the dead ... Limp robes, metallic slippers ... The rosary is carried against the breast and makes no sound. At noon the sun shines down liquid and leaden like a yellow splash of water during old-time carnival. The streetcars carry their cargo of hats. Ah, the wind, such joy in this sea of gravity. The *Crónica* and *Comercio* newspapers are blown about until the cart threatens to roll backwards into an oblique flight over rails and pole. A tollbooth jumps to safety. The cart is stopped by the repair shop, like a rolling ball in the classroom by the teacher.

THE AFTERNOON, FOR THE LAST TIME. NOW WE ARE crossing the Plazuela de San Francisco accompanied by the clipped tolling of bells for novena. A wall that blocks the towers—beautifully ugly—has, on the other hand, three picture windows of sleepy blue crystal illuminated by glimpses of the facing sky. This street leads to the sea: a sea no one sees, just like in the major ports. It is not today that we cross the Plazuela de San Francisco; it was yesterday while you were telling me how the twilight hurt your eyes. You were chewing on a hedgerow leaf and rubbing the fingernails of one hand against those of the other. I feared hearing your secrets—always sincere—so, to prevent you from speaking, I recalled out loud a distant afternoon that, like in a joke, was a huge fried egg, an embossed sun of brilliant gold almost on the periphery of the rugged and aqueous porcelain sky, a nutritive afternoon that stained gluttonous poets from their foreheads to their noses with sunset hues. Movie houses bleat in their dark and filthy cribs. A turkey vulture, at the top of a flagpole, is a turkey chick—arched blackness and gray beak. An old woman walked aimlessly along the esplanade, then took off dramatically to who knows where. An automobile turned on one headlight, revealing one cone of drizzle. We felt the cold on our eyelids. Yesterday ... Bass Street now consoles us with its shadowy alcoves, its pharmaceutical smells of eucalyptus, its medicinal words, its rows of consumptive trees. And there is nobody who isn't you or I.

RAMÓN PUT ON HIS GLASSES, AND HIS FACE AND LEGS looked more negroid than ever. He said yes and filled his pockets with his hands. A bright star quivered in the sky; another star trembled closer by. The sky was night blue, with strands of day, with threads of day, feminine, seamstressy. The scissors of wind sounded as in a barbershop, and it was difficult to know if one's own hair or the Chinese silk of the sky was being cut. With humility Ramón divested himself of hope, the way he would have divested himself of his hat. Life, and he who was beginning to live ... One must resign oneself, he said, quoting Schopenhauer, then breathed deeply, as if asleep. I preferred Kempis to Schopenhauer. Nietzsche was a farce. Ramón had not read Nietzsche, but he had heard of the Superman. He knew that Superman was an alias of Firpo. He was beginning to live ... Obligatory military service ... A possible war ... Children, inevitable ... Old age ... The daily grind ... I whispered to him delicately, words of consolation, but I failed to console him; he hunched his shoulders and knit his brow; he rested his elbows on his knees; he was a failure. At sixteen years old! ... Oh, to think what had befallen him! He almost cried; a spinster on a bicycle stopped him short. A bright star crackled in the sky; another one was extinguished closer by.

11

A dog, vagrant and mongrel, watched us walking, looking back. I spelled out the words for him with my fingers: "It's nothing. Don't be a pest." We went to Lima. The automobile tires sparked along the sticky asphalt; a flash of golden satin at the end of each block; the telephone poles mirrored one another perfectly; the pigeons were still heralding the morning. We returned to Barranco at night.

THIS ONE WAS AN ENGLISHMAN WHO FISHED WITH A rod. A high, thick nose on his long terra-cotta face; below, the mouth of a priest, drawn and still, the lips sunken; and a cigar from Catacaos; and one shaved hand; and a long, long, long rod … Undoubtedly, this Englishman was like all fishermen, an idiot, yet his legs did not sway; instead, he stood upon that support rail as slippery as moss-covered tiles. What was this English-man fishing for, a careless *lampo* or minuscule *tramboyos*? I think he spent hour after hour fishing for a piece of seaweed with a drop of water on its tail that swelled and then collapsed before he could catch it. A poet? Nothing of the sort: a travel agent from Dawson and Brothers Ltd., but he fished with a rod. And the temptation to push him—and the Catacaos floating—and the rod driven into the sandy bottom like a topmast …

IN THE BEWITCHED MIRROR OF THE RAINY STREET —
a drop of milk, the streetlamp's iridescent globe; a drop of water, the sky above; a drop of blood, one's self with this foolish
joy at winter's unannounced arrival ... I am now that man with
no age or race who appears in geography monographs, with
ridiculous clothes, a somber face, his arms spread wide as he ar-
ranges India ink pastures and charcoal clouds—the engraving's
sparse, ragged landscape. Here is the West; North on that wall;
South behind me. That way to Asia. This way, Africa. Everything
beyond the sierra or the sea suddenly approaches, meridian by
meridian, in a man, upon the brown waters of the causeway.
The Turk is the Levant and the Occident, a tightly bound sheaf
of latitudes: the face is Spanish; the pants, French; the nose, Ro-
man; the eyes, German; the tie, Belgian; the bales of hay, Russian; the restlessness, Jewish ... As we travel to the East, the
numbers increase. To the West, they decrease. Dakar or Peking.
A haremesque joy as the blue cloth appears through the lattice
with its drab edges of black rubber. The fields, with their rash of
ancient burial grounds, at the road's open mouth. Fading light of
falling drizzle. Trees with wet birds. There is a reason the earth
is round ... And these cars, soiled by haste, by pride, by mud

… The fig trees make the houses grow in the illusion of muddy and mossy foliage, almost water, almost water, water above, and below, sediments, chlorophyllous and clay, I don't know … Swallows, grasshoppers. One might even open one's round, ichthyological eyes. In the water, under water, the lines break up, the reflections are at the mercy of the surface. No, at the mercy of the force that moves it. But it's the same thing, after all. Asphalt pavement, a fine and fragile mica sheet … A very narrow street widens then contracts from beginning to end like a pharynx so that two vehicles—one cart and a second cart—can continue together side by side. Everything is thus: tremulous, dark, as if on a movie screen.

RAMÓN NEVER THOUGHT THAT A MINUSCULE, BARREN jacaranda tree looked like an Englishwoman with glasses. A somewhat crazy photophobic gringa photographer—the delight of a rooming house with cretonne drapes and clean lace curtains—wandered around Barranco day and night in vain. The gringa was a roaming road, blinded by the sun, leading to the tundra, to a country of snow and moss where a gaunt, gray city of skyscrapers loomed as mysterious as the machinery in a dark factory. Miss Annie Doll's life had to be loaded onto a sleigh and an airplane, an automobile and a transatlantic liner. And in the end, Miss Annie Doll was a ruddy infant suckled on a sterilized bottle. Synthetic milk, canned meat, hard liquor, seven years in a sports academy, reindeer and squirrels, trips to China, archaeological collections in a suitcase from Manchester that holds all of civilization, aspirin tablets, the smell of sawdust in hotel dining rooms, the smell of smoke on the high seas, on board ... You evoke so many things, photophobic gringa photographer, you who live in a rooming house, an enormous building with its third floor of gray planks, with its sadness of a railroad station and a chicken coop! Gringa: sheltered road leading to the tundra, to Vladivostok, to Montreal, to the South Pole, to the perpetual winter of whitewashed scientific academies, to anywhere at all …

But Ramón does not see your image spread into the jacaranda by the sun. To him, you are a somewhat crazy gringa, and a jacaranda is a tree that produces many purple flowers. You are a red, long, sinewy mobile thing that carries a Kodak over its shoulder and asks questions that are wise, useless, and nonsensical … A jacaranda is a solemn, old-fashioned, confidential, expressive, gaudy, mindful, family tree. You: almost a woman; a jacaranda: almost a man. You: human, in spite of everything; it: a tree, when we leave off the poetry.

Ramón, I'm not thinking about those splendid jacarandas in the park. Miss Annie Doll's only relationship to them is as their antithesis: a vegetable antithesis full of nature and supreme truth. But there stands a jacaranda on a secluded street that smells of bananas: a zigzagging street full of laundries; an alleyway lined with whitewashed walls without windows or doors that have the aura of a military hospital or a recently inaugurated school building. And the jacaranda on that street is the one I say is the gringa, or I don't know if it is a jacaranda that is the gringa or if it is the gringa that is a jacaranda. Whether the tree is very young or very old, I don't know. Facing it we have the same doubts as when we face pieces of pottery in museums, not knowing if they are from Nasca or Chimu, authentic or forged, black or white. Perhaps the jacaranda on Mott Street is both young and old at the same time, like the gringa—lanky, almost completely naked, with just one foliated arm, one stump of purple flowers, free, as if blown there by the wind. Remember, Ramón. We have gone, many an afternoon, to Mott Street to hear the church bells ring for evening Angelus: iridescent soap bubbles that immature

Saint Francis shoots through blowpipes from the church towers into a child's sky. Ramón, don't you remember how the bells
would burst above us; how they gave neither sound nor sight,
just the cold smell of water, much too brief and bright for us to
notice at the moment it wet our faces, which were turned toward
the darkening sky? The sunset was an overripe banana behind
the Elysian bananas of Mott Street. But let's forget about the
jacaranda and the church bells of Saint Francis. Let's remember
Miss Annie Doll, tourist and photographer, a spring dressed in a
jersey that sprang out of this Peruvian resort town's box of sur-
prises. You pushed a button, and Miss Annie Doll thrust out her
body and a pair of yellow glasses. The toy was a local attraction,
not for sale; it belonged to everyone, thoroughly public. The
city and Miss Annie Doll … She lived on an income that came
from far away, like a box of tea; she spoke a Latin that broke her
clean porcelain teeth into a thousand smithereens like crystals;
she failed to understand the bells of Saint Francis because she
took to hearing them in Hebrew, and Saint Francis did not know
any dead languages, only how to blow soap bubbles to cheer
up God; she wore glasses with the same tortoiseshell frames as
yours, only the lenses in hers were yellow, antireflective. And
you, Ramón, are not a high-strung boy, nor do you suffer from
conjunctivitis. Ramón, a normal boy … But the gringa, whether
you like it or not, essentially … I guess … looks like the jacaranda
on Mott Street.

ON THE STREETCAR. SEVEN-THIRTY IN THE MORNING. Below the lowered shades, a glimpse of the sun. Tobacco smoke. An upright old lady. Two unshaven priests. Two shop clerks. Four typists, their laps full of notebooks. One schoolboy: I. Another schoolboy: Ramón. The smell of beds and creosote. The color of the sun settles on the windowpanes from outside, like a cloud of pale translucent butterflies. A sudden excess of passengers. A sinister old lady with skin like crepe, the same crepe of her shawl, where Ramón was sitting. Ramón, hanging from a door—the driver's door—turns his head and his eyes in opposite directions. Ramón's glasses reflect a meek philosophical splendor. Ramón carries the last afternoon—yesterday afternoon—in his satchel. He is going to school because he is late, and he is late because he is going to school. I go with him, near him, secretly chagrined that my feet may not reach the ground. Yet, on the contrary, I can hold in my oversized hand the spines of all my textbooks. And this is a pleasure, almost a consolation, at my pedantic fourteen years of age. My life hangs from the score on my first test as a crumb of bread hangs from a spider's web. Ramón suddenly reaches over a bald head to hand me an engraving of an angel with a constipated look on its face and a twilight that is, first and foremost, roguish. A gift from Catita: eenie, meenie, miney, mo, boarding school silliness, nuns frolicking, and a long jump rope that creates ellipses of afternoon. Catita, date of a desert palm tree … But the gentleman enjoys dates only from the palm trees pruned by "Mamère": the only dates the unlikely Mr. Chaplain graciously accepts come in a small basket with a perfect white silk bow tied to the handle: lying butterflying, that unlikely Mr. Chaplain. Innocent dates, Palestinian dates … The outskirts of Lima. An oil factory swells its greasy belly and belches like a drunk old lady: Lima. In the morning with depths of blue, the uniformed policemen toss back and forth a whistle in diapers, and it screeches and covers its eyes with its fists. Suddenly, the shadow of the school building gets in my eyes like the night.

MY FIRST LOVE WAS TWELVE YEARS OLD AND HAD black fingernails. In that village with eleven thousand inhabitants and a publicity agent for a priest, my then Russian soul rescued the ugliest girl from her solitude with a grave, social, somber love like the closing session of an international workers' congress. My love was vast, dark, sluggish, with a beard, glasses, and portfolios, with sudden incidents, twelve languages, police ambushes, problems from everywhere. She would say to me, when things became sexual, "You are a socialist." And her little soul—that of a pupil of European nuns—opened like a personal prayer book to the page about mortal sin.

My first love left me, repelled by my socialism and my foolishness. "I hope you all don't end up socialists …" And she swore she'd give herself to the first true Christian who came her way, even if he wasn't yet twelve years old. Once alone, I gave up on my transcendent problems and fell truly in love with my first love. I felt a toxicomaniacal, agonizing need to inhale her scent until my lungs burst: the scent of a small school, of India ink, of enclosed spaces, of sun on the patio, of government-issued paper, of aniline, of coarse cotton cloth worn against the skin—the smell of India ink, skinny and black—almost an ebony drawing pen, a ghost of the holidays ... And that was my first love.

My second love was fifteen years old. A crybaby with missing teeth, with braids of hemp, with freckles all over her body, without family, without ideas, with too much future; excessively feminine. My rival was a celluloid and rag doll with stupid, rascally jowls that did nothing but laugh at me. I had to understand an endless amount of perfectly unintelligible things. I had to say an endless amount of perfectly unsayable things. I had to get one hundreds on my exams—a suspect, shameful, ridiculous score; the chicken before the egg. I had to see her, imitate her dolls. I had to hear her cry for me. I had to suck on candies of every color and flavor ... My second love abandoned me like in a tango: "An evil man ..."

My third love had beautiful eyes and legs that were very coquettish, almost cocotte. Required reading was Friar Luis de León and Carolina Invernizio. Wayward girl ... I can't imagine why she fell in love with me. I consoled myself with the twelve spelling errors in her last letter for her irrevocable decision to be my friend after almost being my lover.

My fourth love was Catita.

My fifth love was a dirty girl with whom I sinned almost at night, almost in the sea. The memory of her smells as she smelled, of shadows in a movie theater, of a wet dog, of underwear, of sweets, of hot bread—overlapping odors and each on its own almost disagreeable, like frosting on cakes, ginger, meringue, et cetera. The collection of smells made of her a true temptation for a seminary student. Dirty, dirty, dirty ... My first mortal sin ...

THE PORT REMAINED BEHIND, WITH ITS NECKLACE OF lights and its husky silhouette of love for a man who is serious and not a spendthrift. Fifty thousand souls and a distant, very distant joy on the other side of the port—the enormous curve of the sea, the Panama Canal, the Atlantic Ocean, Grace Liners, and the et ceteras of destiny. Suddenly—he knew not how—Paris. And sixty chapters of a novel he had been writing on board: one thousand pages blackened by letters that threatened Manuel's sanity, mad things, shouting, and all without motive. His jacket stiffened and tensed at that bundle of conflict and hysteria. Because the novel was a conflict of hysterias—a woman threw herself into the arms of a millionaire, and he bit her chin. Astral autobiography; I suppose … A silent bus made of springs and elastic bands carried Manuel to the hotel through the darkness at breathless speed. A gust of fog, cold, drizzle, and gasoline blew the curtain and left upon the windowsill the whiff of a phonograph—rubber, adultery, home remedies … That's how a stork would have left a child in an unmarried woman's bed: a mistake, out of fatigue, as a joke … Like in Barranco, no more and no less. He got undressed. Once naked, he did not know what to do; he wanted to go out, return to Lima, do nothing. He got into bed—early, bored and indolent—and fell fast asleep. In a moment he was back in Lima, on the Jirón de la Unión, at twelve noon. Ramón was carried through side streets in a mud-splattered Hudson that had frighteningly shaky, half-crazed windows. An ambulatory fig tree strolled down a street crowded with seminarians, streetwalkers, and geometry professors—a thousand aging gentlemen, dirty collars, sticky fingers. Manuel awoke, and now it was Paris with its smell of asphalt and its factory sounds and its public pleasures. Manuel visited the Latin American consulates; in the Louvre, under the grotesqueries of colors, a sentimental cocotte left one of her rough and dry hands between both of his cadaverous ones; he sinned twice at the Moulin Rouge; on the Pont Alexandre III, a star from Lima smiled at him on the edge of the brim of his hat. And one day—he did not know how—he awoke in Lima, wrapped in his sky-blue blanket, those silly wings tucked under his guardian angel. Now it was Lima with its smell of sun and guano and its private pleasures. Manuel did not know what to do: return to Paris, go out, do nothing ... So he fell back into a deep sleep.

THE SLOPE OF THE CLIFF PLUNGED INTO FIG TREES, moist earth, trenches, moss, vines, Japanese pavilions: from top to bottom, from the parish church to the beach. Suddenly, the sinister, rampant road twisted. And riding a covered sled—on one side, light; on the other, a make-believe cavern and an invisible madonna and a miracle of candles that stay lit under drips— it fell onto the platform. An old-time tenderness played pieces of Dunker Lavalle on the piano, and a violin hid its voice behind an obese, unknown Italian millionaire. An old man, down below, in the sea, sprinkled those interested in his bald spot with the water that flowed down his hands out of his round, hollow arms; and the old man was a suction pump and two parish priestly hands, forgiving and jovial. Here one might want to hang signs on the indifferent doors covered with blinds: "No Sinning in the Hallways." "Bathers Are Asked to Refrain from Speaking English." "Total Destruction of the Place Is Not Permitted." "Et cetera." Here one is possessed by a certain kind of frenetic and infantile, experienced and weary, critical and dilettantish culture. Paul Morand on a sailing boat accompanied by his earless, raceless lover on their way to Siam, as in the social pages of the newspaper. Cendrars, who comes to Peru to preach the enthusiasms of a spontaneous Bavarian explorer (lynched tourists, wheat plantations, and the man who strangles his destiny). Radiquet: carrying around on tiptoe his sweetheart who is suddenly made ugly by a heroic husband. Istrati: reeking of Dutch cheese, a ship's hold, Eurasian misery. All the same, all indistinct, unclassifiable—secretaries of embassies, heirs to textile mills, day students at schools run by European nuns, failed university students; devout women who have come for their health, for a saintly scandal, a spiritual experience. An excessive Baedeker, a guide from who knows which avant-garde Pentapolis, inadmissible nationalism, a great big hunch ... A drunken Charleston shakes a buxom lady as if she were a sack full of wood chips. A policeman rubs his anointed and cunning hands. The funicular lends a modern flourish to the cliff's pre-republican calling. Lima, Lima, finally ... And everything is nothing but your insanity and a Peruvian resort for bathing in the sea. And a native and premature desire that Europe will make of us men, women's men, terrible Portuguese men, men like Adolphe Menjou, with a false mustache and a valet, with an international smile and a dozen London gestures, with specific danger and a thousand unexpected vices, with two Rolls-Royces and a German liver ailment. Nothing else. Bad Nauheim, Cauterers, summer in Paris ... Nothing of the sort.

SHE WORE A PAROCHIAL-SCHOOL BLOUSE AND HAD A very polite index finger. Public-school teacher. Twenty-eight years old. Perfect health. Christian resignation to spinsterhood. A very white face. A very fragile nose. And a pair of little glasses attached to her right ear with a delicate gold chain. And, above all, Reuter Soap—a white, pedagogical smell. The skin on her nose was finer and more sensitive than that on any other part of her body, and though no one could actually prove this, it was nevertheless true. The truth!—the enthusiasm of a missionary priest, the theme of a frantic cuckold, the worst part of a good book—anything except the skin of a twenty-eight-year-old pedagogue. Right? Her nose filled her glasses full of difficulties: they became a lap dog that barked out reflections. Modern manners and the news in *La Prensa* made her nose wrinkle, but less, less … At seven in the morning her face blossomed—unusual, unexpected flower—a begonia plant in a green pot in her window, on her windowsill, in her house, in her house, in her house. "Eeny, meeny, miny, mo" … Then her face ended just above the long, sturdy, firm body of a guardian angel, a prudent virgin, a voluntary Miss. With an awkward rustle of sheets in her chamber—the silly, useless fluttering of a caged goose—the daily life of Miss Muler began, the antithesis of a treasurer, a woman of her house—domestic, girlish, soft, intimate, and cold like a pillow at six o'clock postmeridian. Miss Muler did everything well: with silence, indifference, reluctance. At breakfast she held her cup between her thumb and index finger, as if she were on a date, and her whole hand turned into a vital, hard, intelligent claw And her index finger, more crooked than ever, acquired virtue, exoticism, smiles, the sadness of a Russian former duke waiting tables in Berlin. At the stroke of nine in the morning, Miss Muler instantly became a public-school teacher, basic education, a pillar of the state; she said no and made her hands into a little ball. In the afternoon, Miss Muler submitted herself to sounds, sights, and scents, and spun poetry with the wingtips of her legs and arms, ivory forever brand new as in the gums of an elephant. Nonsensical possibilities from an old maid: ubiquity, crown and scepter, a heavenly meadow, to be a bird with the head of a carnation, to die a saint, to go to Paris ... Asleep, she dreamed of Napoleon riding a green horse and of Saint Rosa of Lima. She cried only when she had a handkerchief. She would say, "Bon Dieu," and lackadaisically let out a rippling laugh. She did not understand Eguren, but she recognized him when she saw him. She would mumble, "Out of the question" ... her eyes far away. And, "My pleasure." And, "Jesus, Jesus ..." She would place half her finger perpendicular over the page of the book she was reading. Et cetera. Miss Muler dreamed about him one night, three days after having met him. His turn came before Ramón's; a colonel who fought in the War of the Pacific—a patriotic dream from a nationalistic textbook. Ramón had finally penetrated Miss Muler's subconscious; and one night my favorite friend became a priest; he hailed from Palestine on Mister Kakison's back. Lima turned into a tangled heap of towers; the ringing of bells fell like stones in a labyrinth of dirt clods; an Italian angel sang in Latin; a Boy Scout trumpet called only to men of good will; the Jordan River escaped while laughing at the sky through the squinting eye of Viceroy Superunda's congenial bridge; Ramón, wearing the habit of the Order of Mercy and with the moon of Barranco in his hands, appeased the elements and coughed horribly. Miss Muler fell in love with Ramón. Ramón did not fall in love with Miss Muler. Miss Muler was twenty-eight years old; Ramón, eighteen. But, in spite of it all, Ramón did not fall in love with Miss Muler. From a million points of view, in a tango as long as a movie reel, the phonograph filmed the resort town in slow motion—yellowed and desolate like a Mexican village in a cowboyish comic book with Tom Mix. And, behind it all, the sea, useless and absurd like a bandstand the morning after the afternoon of a gymkhana. And a triangle of common pigeons carried off Miss Muler's pen strokes in their beaks, romantically.

A GERMAN WEARING THICK-SOLED SHOES AND SMELL-
ing of leather and disinfectant rented a room full of spiderwebs
in Ramón's house. There was another one, freshly wallpapered
and also to let, but the one with spiderwebs had a large window
facing the neighbor's garden that looked out on elder trees and
a plaster of Paris Eros with a terrible parrot perched on its head.
A swallow that was hunting fleas between the floorboards when
Herr Oswald Teller, with rapt attention, looked over the room
for the first time with the round magnifying glass on his forehead convinced him to rent it without delay, fearing that some
Herr Hemmer or another Herr Dabermann would find out that
a room with swallows and a garden with plaster love and sea
breezes was for rent. The morning after that afternoon, Ramón's
sleep-filled and unbespectacled eyes saw descend from the cart
the portrait of Bismarck, the violin, the gaiters, the rucksack, the
seven languages, the microscope, the crucifix, the mug for Herr
Oswald Teller's beer, for he was changing his place of residence
mit Kind und Kegel, with all his belongings. Finally Herr Oswald
Teller himself, fat and wet like the morning, descended from the
cart. He walked along beside it, his tiny legs getting tangled in
the tail bristles of the mule that pulled the flatbed cart. Martinita:

an enormous old mule, fussy as an in-law ... And Herr Oswald
Teller spoke to the cart driver about mornings in Hanover, the
full moon, the industrialization of America, the Battle of the
Marne ... and his *rr*'s rose from his belly, and his glances flowed
from his brain, and his memories skated around on bluish snow.
And Herr Oswald Teller abruptly stopped talking when Martinita abruptly stopped pulling. Joaquín, as sullen and hermetic as
a Javanese idol, chewed with his black jaws and imagined the sea,
remote and perpendicular, in the sea of fog between his mule's
ears. The fog of the sea smelled of shellfish, and the sea hung
in the fog. Over the sidewalk fell a dark, dense, delicate, brief
rain of German illustrated magazines—*Fliegende Blatter*, *Garten*,
and *Laube*—magazines with covers displaying horrible cosmic
nudes and fierce euphoria over architectural Wagnerian paint-
ing ... Then everything was in Herr Oswald Teller's room. Herr
Oswald Teller found a spot for everything. The cry of a milkmaid
fell unexpectedly into the middle of the room, and a few minutes
later, so did the church bells ringing six times at six o'clock in the
morning. Herr Oswald Teller stuffed the six bells of six in the
morning into the pocket of his hunting jacket, and he grabbed
the cry of the milkmaid with the brush he used to brush his bald
spot. (One day, Herr Oswald Teller told Ramón that when he
brushed his hair he felt happy, smelling the stables and imagin-
ing he was in Hanover; and the milkmaid's cry was still a reflection of country light—blue and peaceful—on the brush.)
In the afternoons, in the long pre-nights to Lima's winter, Herr
Oswald Teller, from his mildewy room, flooded the house with
music and homesickness and geniality. Liquefied Mozart poured
down the staircase and formed puddles in the hollows like a tor-
rent of rain that had soaked through the roof. Ramón fumed.

Classical concert … Brrr … Old music, intransigent, imposed on the admiration of a twenty-year-old, by dint of warnings, horrible grandmotherly warnings full of good sense … And Ramón drifted away in his armchair and stiffened, and listened, and in the end grew dizzy with a magic flute in his eardrums.

LULÚ WORE A ROBE LIKE A CABBAGE LEAF, COOL AND stiff. The colors on her spinster-doll face were too bright. She obviously needed to be allowed to age, to fade. One had the urge to hang her out in the sun by her braid. Lulú was the terror of the parochial lay-sisters—she sowed the benches of the temple with thumbtacks, poured holy water on the faithful, made the sexton fall in love with her, upset the chorus, tripped over everyone's feet, and extinguished all the candles ... And she was good: a pure little soul who sought only to cheer God up with her mischief. Lulú was a saint in her own way. And among the flock of stubborn and stuffy saints in the ecclesiastical mode, Lulú's wild and human saintliness stood out like a bramble over a cauliflower patch.

THE ESPLANADE ATOP THE SEA CLIFF OF BARRANCO,
the last stretch on the way to Chorrillos, zigzagging, seascape
in relief, carved with a knife, a sailor's toy, so different from the
esplanade of Chorrillos: too much light, an excessive horizon,
obese sky undergoing the sea's cure. The esplanade of Chorrillos: superpanorama with a fourth dimension: solitude … And the
whole sea changes along with the esplanade—this one, a transatlantic cruise; that one, route to Asia; the other, first love. And the
sea is one of Salgari's rivers or Loti's shores, or Verne's fantastic
ships, and the sea is never glaucous but rather has pale, colorless
zones, lined with the tracks of ducks, full of minute coasts and
feeble backgrounds. The sea is a soul we once had, that we cannot
find, that we barely remember as our own, a soul that is always
different along every esplanade. And the sea is never the cold
and vigorous one that squeezed us, with estival lust, throughout
our childhood and our vacations. The esplanade is full of German shepherds and English nursemaids, a domestic sea, family
stories, the great-grandfather was captain of a frigate, or a free-
booter in the sea of the Antilles, a bearded millionaire. An esplanade lined with ancient gardens of fragile roses and dirty and
dwarfed palm trees; a fox terrier barks at the sun; the solitude of

the shacks appears at the windows to contemplate noontime; an unemployed worker, and light—the light of the sea, humid and warm. An esplanade with patches of dry grass, tension before a first date with a girl we didn't really love; above this esplanade is a varied sky that collides with the one over the sea. An esplanade with only one hour of quietude: six o'clock in the afternoon, the two twin skies, one with no chance for continuity, both with the same gulls and melancholies.

AMPLE, HARD, FIRM END-OF-FEBRUARY SUN. THERE
is no shadow possible at this immutable, exact, artificial midday.
Night will never arrive. It is two o'clock in the afternoon, and the
sun is still halfway across the sky, stuck in a stubborn and foolish
affinity for the earth. The plaster along the streets gleams—the
white, the yellow, the light green, the sky blue, the pearly gray—
the perfect, prudent colors of the houses of Barranco. There is
the scent only of heat, only heat—a solid scent of fully dilated
air. Brass and tiles clang in the windows. Flagless poles with
dangling ropes that form knots on top of the cornices. The one
o'clock bell dissolves its dregs of sound in the spongy air, and
over Barranco descends a flutter of schoolchildren: the light and
feathery whiteness of the moment flies off to sea. The end of the
lunch hour that is the solitude of the streets and a silvery hot
and cold silence, and the shimmering of causeways paved with
round, auriferous stones, with stones from riverbeds, thirsty
and gasping. With its squeaking and banging a cart carries off
the fever of all the streets it has traveled through: nightmares,
beings, banana groves, bitterness, deaf systoles and diastoles …
The sultry air isochronally strikes the eardrums of the window
glass—tense, painful membranes. And in the wake of the cart,

the streets remain pale, convalescent, without ailments and without health. And the cart continues past the walls to burn up the evil of the streets in the blaze of the distant sunset. A memory of banana groves ... Each sound collides with the hard air, and there is a bang. Three in the afternoon. And a trolley car sings its heart out with the guitar of the road to Miraflores— gray, convivial, sad, two metal strings, and around its neck, the green belt of the boulevard that churns the sea air. Streetcar, sambo casanova.

SHE SHOUTED AT ME THAT SHE LOVED ME WITH HER
entire face, fresh and covered more than ever with lint from her
towel; naked, cold, and juicy in yellow overalls like the inside
of oranges; she almost fell into my arms—an adverse wind
stopped her; I told her she was as terrifying and inoffensive as a
sea lion; she did not believe me; her gluteal, livid knees trembled;
I reproached her for her impertinence, her immodesty, her bad
faith, her seventeen years, her bare feet that could get hurt; she
warned me that she bit like a *tramboyo* when caught, and she
showed me her fishbowl teeth; she could also scratch, like a
hunted otter—she slowly unsheathed her not-at-all-corneous
nails: misty, opaque; she allowed me not to get frightened; we
went down to the big beach, I think on a rope, like cats on coast-
ing steamboats; we returned to the gazebo in the water; she
measured the craziness in my eyes with her own; with a frown
she tightened the straps of her nakedness over her pale shoulders; she was trying to say to me, as if to a naughty child, "Settle
down, or there'll be no treats …," but she was afraid of making
me cry. My thorax—that of a studious boy—distracted her from
my words; she forgave me; she became natural; the cold x-rayed
her thighs and bound her arms together; she looked out beyond

43

the round pier; suddenly—tracing a stupendous, incomprehensible parabola—she threw herself into the bather's semi-sea, head first behind her inverted wig that hung like the tentacles of an octopus on a grappling iron in the market. I had to wait for her on the beach, under the terrace—the semidarkness of a marine cavern—amid wholesalers—hairy, vertical, shivering cetaceans—and the stench of seafood—green vapors; she emerged from her drenching dressed in water; she no longer loved me; the two of us, under the platform; I thought of a caustic and pretty jellyfish, but no …; I grabbed her hand that was as slippery as a fish; I dragged her along toward the light and the desert in a painful race over round pebbles; my heels grew numb; our entwined hands crashed into a useless rail standing upright with a stupid rock balanced on its tip, and we separated; she wanted to be a rail that could not be dragged along the beach, just like that; a mercurial lizard carried away one of her sad glances; she wanted to forgive me with all her heart and I would not allow it; her garment of moisture fell; she hit the beach with her knees and said no …

THIS AFTERNOON, THE WORLD IS A POTATO IN A sack. The sack is a small, white, dusty sky, like the small sacks used for carrying flour. The world is little, dark, gritty, as if just harvested in some unknown agricultural infinity. I have gone to the countryside to see the clouds and the alfalfa fields. But I have gone almost at night, and I will no longer be able to smell the scents of the afternoon, tactile scents, that are smelled through the skin. The sky—affiliated with the avant-garde—creates out of its dusty whiteness round, multicolored clouds that at times look like German balls and at others, really, like the clouds of Norah Borges. Now I must smell colors. And the road I take turns into a crossroads. And the four pathways born to the road screech like newborn babes: they want to be rocked; and the wind turns into a swinging young dandy after nightfall and does not want to rock roads: the air wears oxford trousers, and there is no way to convince it that it is not a man. I walk away from the sky. And, as I leave the countryside that is hemmed in by urbanizations, I notice that the countryside is in the sky: a flock of fat, fleecy clouds, award winners at the Exposition—a romp in the green sky. And this I see from far away, so far away that I get into bed to sweat colors.

AFTERNOONS WERE WHITE IN WINTER, AND IN SUM-
mer, a reddish gold, a growing gold that eventually turned into
a sun, a sun that filled the entire sky. Winter afternoons were
white; the luminous and piercing whiteness of salt crystals, and
the sun therein was a silvery sun with a chipped circumference.
But in March there was a Monday with a pink afternoon, an afternoon of decadence in the style of D'Annunzio, and everybody
was deeply moved by the pink afternoon. Long lines of thin-
blooded old ladies—black scarves wrapped around yellow necks
with red tendons (potbellied old men accompanied by nameless
friends)—the current price of cotton, hairy hands wearing wed-
ding rings, and lenses, and glasses, and spectacles, and spherical
eyelids, and wrinkles that looked painted on. But suddenly, the
pinkness turned red, and the sunset became an everyday sunset,
and the audience at the celestial movie house voiced its disap-
proval at the change of program. Weren't they showing *Divino
amor*? The story was by D'Annunzio; the hero was Fiume's, a
bald dago who wrote verses, an unlikely man, an Italian national
fantasy, an aviator, a wreck, an author in the index, a show not to
be missed ... Valentino ... Dream landscapes ... Passion, sacrifice,
jealousy, a sumptuous wardrobe, high society ... And suddenly,

nothing! The vulgar epic poem of the summer, the red sky, the sun sky, and night as a shout. The respectable audience fiercely stamped its feet as it withdrew in an orderly fashion befitting people who know their rights—serious people, honorable people. Suddenly the sky donned the come-look-and-see attitude of a street vendor, and then there was no sun no summer no anything: just buttocks in the air, enormous buttocks reddened by a lengthy sitting. The audience swore it would appeal to the mayor. On Matti Street, the fig trees went quickly to sleep so they could get up early. At a window, a very old piano was dying of love, like the Duke of Hohenburg—pink bald spot, white sideburns—in one or another of Kalman's operettas.

WE SWAM IN THE SEA AND THE AFTERNOON, TO THE left of the West and concealed by the pier as if it were something the city had forbidden and that could cause the resort to close. Lalá's mother clung to a wave that had broken at high tide, a violent wave, maned and clumsy like a buffalo—the poor woman looked through the foam for one of her hands that had been carried off by the wave. The previous day—a cold, malignant yesterday—it was one of her slippers that had strayed; by the time she noticed her bare foot—when she stepped on an underwater gringo—the shoe was no longer afloat, for it was made of rubber; the gringo's shapeless diver's head surfaced; Lalá's mother apologized; the gringo did not understand; her mother nodded *yes* in English, to herself, quickly, between two crashing waves. Her mother had found her lost hand in those of a nearby and bemused Arab, who shouldn't have been allowed to swim because he was an Arab, et cetera. Lalá showed me the nipple of one of her breasts. I hid in the sea. Lalá could already have been my girlfriend. Her mother rose like a submarine. She simply was not herself in a bathing suit. The legs of the bottoms and the sleeves of the top were puffed up with water. With the purple tip of her tongue she subdued a red lock of wet hair that traversed her face from her hairline to her chin like a scar. The cord of her scapular was wrapped tightly around her shoulder, as if for a bloodletting. The old woman defied the bathhouse, waged war on the sea, and cast a shadow over the shadow under the platform. The ocean-sea descended. Above, in a blue zone of the sky, the waxing moon blinked in time with the frustrated high tide. The stones that had escaped with a horrible din from Lalá's mother's path came to rest at our feet—excited, friendly. The sand rushed underfoot—it wanted to knock us down and carry us out to the high seas as if we were seashells. Lalá stuck her pinkies in her ears; her eyes and teeth chattered. Suddenly, unprovoked—behind a large, sickly, complacent wave that did not advance—I kissed her; the kiss resounded through the afternoon like through a theater. The water was flecked with black and green. The railings of the pier broke up and disintegrated underwater into fillets of shadows, shadows of fish, patches of shadow ... Everything seemed on the verge of collapse: the sky with its horizon in flames; the sea full of tidal eddies; the pier with its girders dissolved into the sea. I did not love Lalá. My fingers were wrinkled, stiff. Lalá blew on them the warm, humid breath of a hairdresser's spray. We emerged from our swim as from bed, as from a dream ... Lalá yawned.

I PICTURE THAT MAN AS AN INDISTINCT UPRIGHT-
ness from which hung a badly cut coat. A few words in Ramón's
diary attempt, in vain, to reconstruct in my mind the destroyed,
dissipated image of the man. "Dog eyes in a face of wax, full of
a sweetness that was nothing but indifference. And one of his
index fingers—on the right hand, the finger of idlers, of canons,
of boys—was rigid, and yellowed by tobacco. And the ashen
moustache with golden handlebars that seemed to burst from
his nasal passages like a heavy cloud of pitch ... And the trousers,
empty holes, with large bulges at the knees ..." So states Ramón's
diary, a black oilskin-covered notebook filled with words that
ended up, I don't know how, in the hands of Miss Muler, precep-
tor and directress of the Republic of Haiti Elementary School.
Ah! Miss Muler's hands ...! How they moved about among the
writing instruments and cardboard grammar books—the rudi-
ments of geography taught with angelic purity and remarkable
self-confidence! But those notes—I don't know if they truly reflected Ramón's image of that man or were simply nonsense that
descended into my friend's fingers while he was writing in his
diary, there transformed into the foolish desire to make a point.
Did that man ever exist? Is it possible that Ramón and I simply

dreamed him up? Might we have created him out of someone else's features and his own gestures? Did that man have memory, understanding, and will? ... Because I can now see the details Ramón mentions arranging themselves in a human form in the atmosphere of a dense and yellow summer. I also see that man dispersed, incomplete, part madness, part environment, part real, with his belly of air and his calves of the marine horizon— vertical, charading, vexed, on the edge of the esplanade without a railing. Perhaps everything is nothing but essential elements, physiognomic dates, crosses and capital letters, the shorthand of a wayfaring observer who at a particular moment re-created in Ramón's fat and well-groomed head the image of that man who did, in fact, exist. I now feel the desire to have that man in front of me so I can ask him some weighty questions, the answers to which would reveal the humanity or inhumanity of the sub-ject: "Do you support Leguia? What brand of cigarettes do you smoke? Do you keep a mistress? Do you suffer from the heat?" If that man answered that he was a monarchist, that he did not smoke because he did not have a narghile, that he loved a pious old woman, that he suffered from the heat only in winter, then I could know for a certainty that we, Ramón and I, had created that man during an hour of idleness and twilight, while the sun rolled silently and quickly through a concave sky, red and green like a Milanese ball. There is no doubt that there are men who are nothing more than their empty trousers. There are children who are nothing but the joy of a sailor's hat: children who are not even the hat they wear. There are women who are barely an artificial hand in a purse made of donkey leather. Priests who are nothing but a wrinkle of their cassock. What might that man be?

POST-MIDDAY, VAPORS OF THE SUN AND FROLIC OF puerile boredom ... Catita, evil heart ... There is nothing to do, nothing to think about, nothing to desire. Catita, evil heart ... But now, Catita, nothing matters to me. A street lit with silence—down it go these eyes of ours, our eyes, heedless and curious children. And we are struck blind. And a whiff of a yaraví ballad with its air of the highlands brings a chill to the street. Afterwards, nothing, not even ourselves—you and I, Fernando, devout face and long pants.

Night, hairy and taciturn dogs ... The dirty desire to climb trees that have bloomed with a star as a joke—a mocking, bantering, bursting star; fig tree, fig, in its autumn of shade. Afraid of the bogeyman with the face of a mother-in-law. Catita, cold bed ... Streets under electric lights, a cart's nightmare, squat houses with fabulous palm trees. And a shattered silence that is a mortal sin.

Immaculate morning with recently washed foliage. From time to time a rural breeze, which seems to come, oddly enough, from the windows, passes by carrying the sweet smell of vegetables. But this is a breeze that escapes at the first corner. And the air returns to its clear, clean, empty state. A pretty native woman with her hard, shiny, damp head of hair—a mud carving—walks along absorbed in her own thoughts, watching her own breasts bounce, tremble, bounce … A cook. Her firm and ugly calves darken her white cotton socks. She left her baby in the kitchen. And she is definitely not thinking about him now: now she is thinking only about herself, about the breasts she sees tremble, bounce. Rarefied air. The trolley cars pass in vain: nothing can be heard.

WE READ THE SPANISH, AND NOBODY BUT THE SPAN-
ish. Only Raul leafed through French, English, and Italian books
in translations by someone named Pérez, or González de Mesa,
or Zapata, or Zapater. This is how, in spite of Belda and Azorín,
we had a picturesque image of world literature. This is how we
learned about the life—eternal like Our Father's—of that poor
Stephen Dedalus, "a man who was interesting and wet his bed."
In this way we found out about the trick played on a good theater director by six characters, how they enticed him to write
and then ended up not existing. This is how we found out about
a young man who tried to be the devil's disciple, as if the devil
would demean himself by teaching. And strange names that
were men—Shaw, Pirandello, Joyce—danced around on the
tip of Raul's tongue—puppets bewitched by an illiterate witch.
To know ourselves ... Stephen Dedalus was not Joyce's Stephen
Dedalus: Stephen Dedalus was, undoubtedly, an ambitious boy
who dreamed of marrying a rich Yankee; a boy who was very
intelligent and had a lot of self-confidence, so much so that he
tricked a whole monastery of Jesuits. As for Pirandello's son, he
held the opinion that it was immoral of the father—a cynical
cuckold—to burden a son, about whom nothing bad was ever

said, with a putative mother. Ramón bit his lip. The devil's disciple was a depraved and stubborn young man, and most likely beardless. We did not have a behaviorist concept of humanity. Joyce? An idiot. Pirandello ...? Another idiot. Shaw ...? A third idiot, even more of an idiot than the first two, what with his historical concept of literature, his bad jokes, and his mania for always going against the grain; and above all, so chaste, so old, and so vegetarian; and above all, Irish, that is to say, English, in spite of the Pope and Home Rule.

All of us, except Raul, were steeped in the Spanish and American moldy literary stew. For, just as on Sancho's Island of Barataria, it is the food of canons and rich men.

Let Wilde be the stuff of the curious who commit sins out of boredom. Let's welcome Don Jacinto Benavente's asexual confidants, with their pointed beards, parabolic bellies, and make-believe trousers; and his fairies, who know how to behave in high society; his women, who commit adultery under orders from their confessors; his perfectly humane and useless lives; his centripetal morals; his clichéd conversations: everything of Benavente's. And likewise with Fernán Caballero's literature, a credulous and blessed literature with ecclesiastical license. The same with Pardo Bazán's—literature that smells of an old lady's closet with vague whiffs of thyme, full of sins that are never committed; such pious intentions this author has! And Pereda's withered and uncouth literature, with his severe, somber, frowning girls that give themselves to men for the love of God. And Pérez Galdós's practical and perilous literature with consumptives and the insane and criminals and the diseased, but whom the reader sees from afar at no risk to himself. And Maetzu's: a table of logarithms that smells of aftershave in which everything fits as if into a handbag from Manchester; everything condensed, of course, and full of ciphers, and as dignified as an English maiden. And Camba's literature: a railroad dialogue of a young man without family, without work, without philosophies. And Father Coloma's, full of prudent and wary angels who constantly cling to their zithers, and courtesans with good dispositions, and advice for Catholic aristocrats. And Baroja's digestions, and Azorín's matinees, and Valle-Inclán's vespers, and Zamacoa's nights. Everything, everything, just like that, as it comes, as it falls, but without inhumanities ...

RAMÓN'S AUNT SWAM FOR A LONG TIME. WITH ONE thick hand she wet her tattered cap, and with the other she subdued the waves. From time to time, a slipper would emerge from her unsinkable bosom: it was a truant foot. She was an old woman who was afraid of the rocks: fat, humid, a good summer vacationer; she arrived at the first sign of heat and left at the last. She rented a rickety cabin with a large window and an enormous window shade. A cat that looked like a Negress and a Negress that looked like a toy ... The parish church behind and a phonograph made of tin and wood. The small patio was a basket full of yellowed papers: Ramón's aunt never read the newspapers. In her polka dot bathrobe, she could hear the band in the plaza from the dining room. An old woman. Fat. She will return in December. Ramón, on the other hand, will never return.

NOW THE SUMMER IS REALLY OVER. SUMMER AND THE pretext of summer—girls with happy legs, priests with dark circles under their eyes, the members of the court, the heat, the holidays. The pretext … The pretexts … Now winter is upon us—an extra-calendrical winter, orthodoxly Bergsonian: movies in twenty chapters. Lima, filthy Lima, equestrian, commercial, athletic, nationalistic, so serious … Now summer is really over. We have come, Lucho and I, to the midway esplanade, the one we have baptized Proust Boulevard. Yes, Proust Boulevard—esplanade, ancient, brave, outstanding—which is not a boulevard on both sides but only on one, and on the other, the psychological immensity of the sea, where stands the house of the Swann family, its door perceived through each and every molecule, the infinitesimal analysis of its emotional probabilities. Trees …? Streetlamps—the trunks of shrubs the light twists and the shadows turn green. At six in the morning, at six in the evening, the streetlamps are the most vegetable thing in the world, in an analytic, synthetic, scientific, passive, decisive, botanical, simple way—the upper edges of the trunks support crystal jars that hold yellow flowers. In the great hothouse of the dawn, in the household furnace of the dusk—dark rays, hyper vegetation, observation, summary, skeleton, truth, exact temperature. But now it is not the sea that is on one side of the street in a French novel; the sea is now the sea of waves and little bits of daydreams for a spinster aunt. And, moreover, its colors—an extremely discreet sunset, the antithesis of a dawn that arrives on tiptoe, a morning almost like a pretty girl, but without a kiss or a sign of the cross. Sunday and morning Mass. The organ spreads through the fog like stones banging together in the water. Today there will be a plenilune, full moon, a starless night with its breach of light in the middle—a whole and glorious navel. We shall not stop coming here at night. In the cup of coffee of the firmament will float, indissoluble and delicate, the lump of sugar of the moon. And all of it will be poetry, my friend. We shall prelive a superlife, perhaps actually a future in which all men will be brothers and abstemious and vegetarians and theosophists and athletes. And that sugar moon will turn into a horrible sweetness in our mouths. And a cloud the color of café au lait: what will it be? It might not be anything. Or perhaps it is a verse of Neruda's. Or perhaps a symbolic coast, Amara's fatherland, Eguren's dream. Or, if you prefer, simply a cloud the color of café au lait—there's got to be a reason we are sixteen years old and have peach fuzz on our upper lips. Tomorrow, a soccer match on the rough conch grass of who knows which field on the outskirts of Lima. Champion with tendinous and hairy mosaic legs, beak of the wingless, Byzantine angel in a cloud of dust—a Romanian emigrant, stenographer-typist of the Dess Company, stock agents . . . And the whole match will be a stupid yet perfect plan of advance—in what appears to be the air—of a hard black ball picked up from the ground by an invisible rubber band. A pathetic, trivial, unlikely, cinematic summer of the newsreels. A Rolls runs off snorting along the paved road like a recently castrated world-renowned Swiss bull. And in that Rolls the summer left for the South Pole, carrying with it the already superseded hope for that silvery October full of gulls—that last October we lived. To be happy for one day ... We have been happy for three whole months. And now, what should we do? Die? ... Now you get sentimental. It is sane to become lyrical when life turns ugly. But it is still the afternoon—a matutinal, naive afternoon with cold hands, with westerly braids, serene and contented like a wife, but a wife who still has the eyes of a bride, yet ... Come on, Lucho, tell tales of Quevedo, of brutal copulations, hasty weddings, the nuns taken by surprise, of chaste Englishwomen ... Say whatever comes to mind, let's play at psychoanalysis, chase old ladies, tell jokes ... Everything, anything but die.

Underwood Poems

HARD AND MAGNIFICENT PROSE OF CITY STREETS
without aesthetic preoccupations.

Through them one walks with the police toward happiness.

The stunted poetry of windows is the secret of seamstresses.

There is no greater happiness than that of a well-dressed man.

Your heart is a horn prohibited by traffic regulations.

The houses ruminate on their oxen-like peace.

If you let it be known that you are a poet, you will be sent to the
police station.

Wipe that enthusiasm out of your eyes.

Automobiles rub your hips, turning their heads. You should believe they are lustful women. In this way you will have your adventure and your smile for after dinner.

The men you stumble over have callous office flesh.

Love is anywhere, but nowhere is it any different.

Workers walk by, their eyes resentful of the afternoon, the city, mankind.

Why did the Czech girl shoot you? You have hoarded nothing but your soul.

The city licks the night like a famished cat.

And you are a happy man, perhaps the only happy man.

You have a shirt and no great thoughts of any kind.

Right now I feel angry at those who accuse and those who console.

Spengler is an asthmatic uncle, and Pirandello is an old fool, almost one of his own characters.

But I mustn't get furious at trifles.

Men have done thousands of things worse than their culture: Victor Hugo's novels, democracy, primary school, et cetera, et cetera, et cetera.

But men are bent on loving one another.

And, as they don't often succeed, they end up hating each other.

Because they do not want to believe that all of it is irremediable.

I suspect the Greek polis of being a brothel one should approach with a revolver.

And the Greeks, in spite of their culture, were happy men.

I have not sinned much, but I already know about such things.

Bertoldo would say these things better, but Bertoldo would not ever say them. He doesn't dig very deep—he's old, wants peace and quiet, and even supports the moderates.

The world is not exactly crazy, just overly decent. There is no way to make it talk when it is drunk. And when it isn't, it either abhors drunkenness or loves its fellow man.

But I honestly don't know what the world is or what mankind is.

I only know that I must be fair and honorable and love my fellow man.

And I love the thousands of men within me who are born and die each instant and do not live at all.

Behold my fellow men.

Justice is a few ugly statues in city squares.

I don't like any of them too much or too little—they are neither gods nor women.

I love the justice of women, who don't wear robes and have no divinity.

As far as honor goes, I am not among the worst.

I eat my bread alone so as not to arouse envy in my neighbor.

I was born in a city, and I don't know how to see the countryside.

I have been spared the sin of longing for it to be mine.

I do, on the other hand, desire heaven.

I am almost a virtuous man, almost a mystic.

I like the colors of the sky because they are definitely not German dyes.

I like to walk through the streets, part dog, part machine, not at all man.

I am not wholly convinced of my own humanity; I do not wish to be like others. I do not want to be happy with the permission of the police.

Now there is a little sun in the streets.

I don't know who has taken it away, what evil man, leaving stains on the ground as if from a slaughtered animal.

A crippled little dog walks by: the only compassion, the only charity, the only love of which I am capable.

Dogs do not have Lenin, and this guarantees them a human though genuine life.

To walk through the streets like Pío Baroja's characters (all a bit doglike).

To chew on bones like Murger's poets, but serenely.

But men have an afterlife.

This is why they devote their lives to loving their fellow man.

They make money to kill useless time, empty time ...

Diogenes is a myth—the humanization of dogs.

The longing great men have to be fully dogs. Little men want to be fully great men: millionaires, sometimes gods.

But these things should be said in a low voice—I am afraid of hearing myself.

I am not a great man—I am a common man who strives for great happiness.

But happiness is not enough to make one happy.

The world is too ugly, and there is no way to make it beautiful.

I can imagine it only as a city full of brothels and factories under the flapping of red flags.

My hands feel delicate.

What am I, what do I want? I am a man and want nothing.

Or, perhaps, to be a man like other men.

You do not have big circles under your eyes.

I want to be happy in a small way. With sweetness, with hope, with dissatisfactions, with limitations, with time, with perfection.

Now I can board a transatlantic liner. And during the crossing fish adventures like fish.

But where would I go?

The world is insufficient for me.

It is too large, and I cannot shred it into little satisfactions as I would like.

Death is only a thought, nothing else, nothing else.

And I want it to be a long delight with its own end, its own quality.

The port, full of fog, is too romantic.

Cythera is a North American resort.

The flesh of Yankees is too fresh, almost cold, almost dead.

The panorama changes at every corner, like in a movie.

The final kiss already echoes through the shadows of a room full of burning cigarettes. But this is not the final scene. That is why the kiss echoes.

Nothing is enough for me, not even death; I want proportion, perfection, satisfaction, delight.

How have I ended up in this forsaken and smoky movie house?

The afternoon will have already ended in the city. And I still feel the afternoon.

I now perfectly remember my innocent years. And all bad thoughts are erased from my soul. I feel like a man who has never sinned.

I have no past and an excess of future.

Let's go home ...

BY THE TIME RAMÓN DIED, HE HAD BEEN LEFT WITH only the vile and spent pleasure of looking under seats in public places: movie theater, streetcar, et cetera. A single deep and empty day, when one rolls unconsciously from hour to hour, comatose, like down a cliff, from stone to stone, rock to rock. The dirty cup of the sky slowly filled with sugar, cold water, and lemon juice—a thirsty cloud licked its lips; Ramón died. Looking under seats ... Ramón became a compulsive smoker. Put out the cigarette, flick off the ash, tease the wind, stretch out an arm, all of which, like a matchmaker, facilitated his enjoyment of surprising his shoes when they were almost in their underwear, or of an after-dinner conversation, or of frittering away a Sunday. Sunday of shoes, shadows under the armchairs, a Saturday behind you, a dim light under the table ... The after-dinner conversation of shoes, a short nap: a bootleg shakes the shoelaces loose; a toe cap yawns; the afternoon wrinkles its hide, tired of walking all morning; the right shoe turns on its side and snores. Shoes in their underwear; the uppers, made of yellow fabric, hang out, intimately, like a shirttail ... Shoes, silent old people, in couples, disappointed spouses, together at the heels, separate at the toes. Their past married life unites them forever and alienates them at the hour when they, he and she, would like to be twenty years old again, the right shoe and the left, the male and the female, the husband and the wife—to be twenty years old and marry badly or take a good lover ... The children's booties and slippers meet above, toe to toe, face to face, almost kissing, behind the folds of the nursemaid's apron. Shoes that are adolescent, elegant, languid, crazy, always misdirected, never decently parallel ... shoes going through the bad years, the awkward age, weak lungs and robust tendencies ... Old shoes, one soul in two bodies and not even loving each other ... Ramón left the above verses typewritten on the index of a book with uncut pages I inherited from him.

Old shoes, one soul—a dirty layer of glue between the sole and the insole—one soul in two bodies—two swollen and rheumatic bodies in a wrinkled hide—only one soul in two bodies ... He and she don't want to face each other.

TERRIBLE DAYS IN WHICH ALL WOMEN ARE ONE SIN-gle woman in a nightdress. Terrible days between the lines of Zamacois, terribly serious ... No, not Paul de Kock, Mister Kakison. Fifteen years old and wearing long pants ...! No, life is very serious—nothing less than a woman wearing a nightdress. Don't you understand me, Mister Kakison? It's possible you will never understand me. Admirable! ... What does one live on in London? That's not the point, Mister Kakison. Every night Marina closes her window wearing her nightdress, but certainly that is not a sin. Why shouldn't she? Marina, hairy legs, an eight-o'clock-in-the-morning bather ... To bathe at eight o'clock in the morning in the sea is to bathe in the cold, in the sky, in the hour. A shower of fog, a massage of chills, sponges of indecision, and the nearby barge—a large marine bird with black, drooping wings of folded nets flies backwards. Hmmm ... Mister Kakison, you must wash the stains of the night off your cinnamon-colored robe with gasoline. Night in the robe of an English accountant of the firm Dasy & Bully ... What do you say to that, Mister Kakison? All right ...? That is not an answer at this hour in this country. Say that I am right, and you will speak the truth. Yes, Mister Kakison, say something, something so sane you will never notice.

A NIGHTTIME STROLL. WE HAVE FOUND A STREET hidden from the sky by dense, serious foliage. Now the sky does not exist; it has been rolled up like a rug, leaving barren the floorboards of space where the worlds walk, high society, slowly, silently, fastidiously. Now I love you as I have never loved you—truly, painfully. I don't know how ... Walking through the street that returns our footsteps and our voices to us as in a cavern ... A streetcar destroys a corner, a borehole of light and sound. For a moment we resound, we vibrate in this region of the night like all things—windows, windows, windows ... Now I can be a hero with a convex and bloody chest. If I kidnapped you now, you would tear out locks of my hair and cry out to indifferent things. You will not do it. I shall not kidnap you, not for anything in the world. I need you in order to be at your side, longing to kidnap you. Woe to the one who realizes his desire! The sea sings in the distance like a chorus that begins to sound like an opera. Suddenly it whispers in my ear like a glass of soda that is losing its gas. A piano is the night—sorrow that is antique, clichéd, with four hands. Now I will tell you how I feel:

"I love you because you love me. Your smallness orients my hope as I search for bliss. If you grew like the trees, I would not know what to desire. You are the measure of my pleasure. You are the measure of my desire. Behind all death is the joy of finding you in an earthly paradise. My love, a little thing that never grows. If a star were to fall, you would catch it, and you would burn your hands. My love has not fallen from the sky, and that's why you do not catch it. You are silly and pretty like all women. You laugh, and your laughter reconciles me with the night.

"Why do you not love me? You simply abandon me to the passing wind and the leaf that falls and the lamp that illuminates, as if by losing me you lose nothing. And my love at this hour is the only thing that pays attention to you. Now there is nothing you perturb except my love that follows you like your shadow, wanting to see your eyes. Love me, even if tomorrow, when you awake, you will no longer remember me. Love me, the hour demands it of you! Woe to the one who disobeys time!"

Beyond the night, the dawning of the morning with its colors and its odors. Beyond the night, the birds' song matures in the future like the fruit of the trees. Beyond the night, your thoughts pick realities to embody. And my love follows you through the skyless night of the street, like the memory of a dog you once had that died.

AT THE END OF A VERY URBAN STREET, THE COUNTRY-
side begins abruptly. From the cabins with their little patios and
palm trees and mounds of bellflowers, the broom bushes fall on
the hillocks of spongy earth, over the adobe walls, across the
monotonous blues of the sky ... Droves of donkeys carry adobe
bricks all day long in a gray cloud of dust. Here, in patches on this
hard and spongy ground, lie the city's future houses with their
tarred roofs, delicate plaster window frames, living rooms with
Victrolas and love secrets, perhaps even with their inhabitants—
prudent mothers and modern girls, daredevil young men and
industrious fathers. The face of a distant aunt can be divined in a
clod of earth—the face of one of those aunts three times removed
who comes for a visit to get a breath of fresh air, drink a glass of
cold water. A very old jacaranda tree—the retired municipal in-
spector of decoration—whiles away the hours, so many, of this
extra afternoon, making a few flowers of such expert perfection
that, once finished, he tosses them away with the impassive non-
chalance of a mandarin in his palace in this hasty suburb. And
on the horizon, the blinding smell of smoke sweeps away the
view of poplars and breast-shaped hillocks—the pale, almost
blue, color of granite. A dove passes low overhead, carrying

in its beak a bell from the parish church, and the bell is a piece of straw for its nest. A native girl pulls on the halter of an enormous mule; and she isn't even yet fifteen years old; and the mule grows stubborn and refuses to move; and the arc of the native girl's fragile body grows tenser and tenser; and the mule braces itself with its front legs; and I want to kidnap this girl and run away with her on the mule to the sierra, so nearby, until its peaks scratch the skin off my nose, making me squint when I stare at her. I would then descend, with the native girl in my arms and the mule between my legs, into a dark chasm full of cacti, with somnambulistic confidence in this happy nightmare ... And the mule has pulled the halter out of the native girl's hands and now runs wild, slouching, and bent in a loud and rapid trot along the road, hugging the wall, not knowing where to go ... And the halter that drags behind in the dust has the clean and perverse irony of a rat's tail ...

I HAVE RECEIVED A LETTER FROM CATITA. SHE SAYS nothing in it except that she would like to see me with a sad face. It is a long, tremulous letter in which a nubile girl pulls love by the ears with those sure, those slow, those surgical fingers women use for torture from the age of fifteen until they deliver their first child … There are women who never conceive, and it is they whom Death fears most, for in order to carry them to the next world, he must wage a fierce battle and the bones of his skeleton are sure to get a severe scratching: spinsters die heroically.

Catita's letter smells of spinsterhood—of incense, dried flowers, soap, plaster, medicine, milk. Emblematic spinsterhood with tortoiseshell glasses and a stiff index finger. A blue bun gives the final touch to her appearance—always inevitably partial. A lapdog licks the austere perfume exuded by the silk lace of the blouse. And a blouse of poetic fabrics—a robe of madapollam. And moreover—this, an indispensable detail—a long face whose features—both hard and weak, rough and useless—make a face out of buckram folds. Perhaps a parrot that knows the Litany of Loreto … Perhaps the portrait of an unlikely suitor … Perhaps an obsession to know everything … Perhaps a virtue crowned with thorns ... But Catita is not even fifteen years old. The truth is, there is no reason her fingers should know how to pull on ears. Who knows if some boy, mad with love, doesn't already want to marry her? Catita, taster of young boys, a bad woman who already has the hands of a spinster before the age of fifteen ... English spinster, expert in explosives—propaganda department; a strange, short man; dry, veined hands ... Is that how you'd like to be, Catita? What am I supposed to do with your letter? At this hour it is the impossible of all impossibilities for me to be sad. I am happy at this hour—it's a habit of mine. A fishing boat off the coast of Miraflores waves with its white handkerchief of a sail—so useless in this still, pretty atmosphere, as if painted by a second-rate artist. This greeting is a greeting to nobody, and that happiness, a happiness of nonsense, of small-ness, of regress, of humility ... My cigarette draws admirably, and it is the rejoicing of a youthful fire with blue and minuscule rings and balls; and it is the rural peace of the smell of burned brambles. You see, Catita? You don't see anything because you are not with me on the esplanade above the sea; but I swear to you that it is just as I say. In the afternoon, facing the sea, my soul becomes good, small, silly, human, and is gladdened by the fish-ing boats that unfurl their joke of a sail, and by the burning em-ber of a cigarette—a red-haired child who loses his head in a blue toy shop. And high-flying gulls—black flies in the sky's mug of watery milk—make me want to shoo them away with my hands. When I was five years old and didn't want to drink my milk, I would drown flies in it, then trap them with a spoon—a net compressed by the light until it hardened; and the flies in the milk turned into propellers. And now, suddenly, I feel like a naughty child, and I refuse to drink the glass of milk of the sky because it has no sugar in it. And my Mother Totuca, sweet ebony Buddha, might come along with the sugar bowl painted with a boy monkey dressed as a pirate and a girl monkey dressed as a Dutch girl, together making reverential gestures over the blue band stretching around the bowl's belly ... . Perhaps your star would become sweeter if I sweetened the sky with sugar—your star: so bitter; your star: a spinster who falls in love with impossible comets; your star: leading you down the wrong path of love. Did you hear, Catita? I cannot be sad at this hour—this hour, the only one of the day when I am happy unknowingly, like a child; my hour of foolishness; my hour, Catita. You tasted Ramón, and he did not taste bad to you. Well, okay, so I will be Ramón. I will take upon myself his duty of kissing you on your wrists and looking at you with stupid eyes, worthy of all Ramón's sayings. Foolish and large-winged duty accepted at an insular, celestial, windy, open, desolate hour. I will be Ramón for one month, two months, for however long you can love Ramón. But no: Ramón is dead, and Ramón's face was never sad, and above all, you have already tasted Ramón. Yes, Catita, it's true, but I am not a sad man. As I am at this hour, foolish and happy, so I am most of the day. I am a cheerful boy. I was born with a happy mouth. My life is a mouth that speaks, that eats, that smiles. I don't believe in astrology. I accept that there are sad stars and happy stars. I even assert that sad stars are an excellent motive for writing sonnets with lines of fourteen syllables. But I do not believe our lives have any relationship whatsoever to stars. Oh, Catita! Life is not a river that flows: life is a puddle that stagnates. During the day, the same trees, the same sky, the same day is reflected in it. At night—always the same stars, the same moon, the same night. Sometimes an unknown face—a boy, a poet, a

woman—is reflected in it—the older the puddle, the murkier—
and then the face disappears because a face will not contemplate
itself eternally in a puddle. And the face does contemplate itself.
And the puddle is a turbid and interceding mirror. And an old
man is a puddle in which no young girl would look at herself.
Because one's own life is a puddle, but the lives of others are
faces that come to look at themselves in it. Yes, Catita. But some
lives are not puddles, but rather a lake, a sea, an ocean wherein
only the sky and the mountains, the clouds, the great ships can
be seen. Thus the life of Walt Whitman—a Yankee who was half
crazy and therefore an excellent poet—was an ocean full of
transatlantic liners; Napoleon's, on the other hand, was an ocean
full of warships and cetaceans. Saint Francis's was a trough from
which a donkey with a dove perched on its forehead drank. Phillip II's: a dead sea with a very sad face and sinister legends. Puc-
cini's: an alpine lake, white with canoes from the Cook Travel
Agency. Bolivar's: a dangerous and frightening channel with
reefs and floating casks. Your life: a washbasin in which one
soaks an armful of broom that has the color and smell of sulfur.
Thus is the soul, Catita—either enemy waters or stupid waters—lake, sea, swamp, washbasin full of water. But never a flow
with a current and a bed. My life is a hole dug with the hands of
a truant child in the sands of a beach—a malignant and tiny hole
that distorts the reflections of gentlemen who scold truant children, the image of respectable gentlemen who come to the
beach and infest the sea air—so clean, so brilliant—with their
horrible office odors. Such is my life, Catita—a little puddle on
a beach—so now you see why I cannot be sad. The high tide
undoes me, but another truant child digs me again at the other
end of the beach, and I cease to exist for a few days, during which

time I learn, always anew, the joy of not existing and the joy of resuscitating. And I am the truant child who digs his life in the sands of the beach. And I know the insanity of setting life up against destiny, because destiny is nothing but the desire we feel alternately to die and to resuscitate. For me the horror of death is nothing but the certainty of never being able to resuscitate again, that eternal boredom of being dead. Oh, Catita, don't read sad books, and don't read the happy ones either! There is no happiness greater than being a little hole full of seawater on a beach, a hole destroyed by the high tide, a little hole full of seawater where a paper boat floats. To live is nothing but being a truant child who makes and unmakes his life in the sands of the beach, and there is no pain greater than being a hole full of seawater on a beach that is bored of being one, or of being one that is too easily undone. Catita, don't read destiny in the stars. They know as little about it as you do. Sometimes the puddle of my life coincides with the fall of one of them, and I have had more than one, whole and sincere, in my drop of water. Catita, the stars know nothing about issues that concern girls. They themselves are perhaps nothing but girls with boyfriends, with mothers, and with spiritual addresses. What you decipher in them is nothing but your own concerns, your own joys, your own sadnesses. Moreover, stars have a much too provincial beauty; I don't know ... too naive, too real ... The poor things imitate your way of viewing things. Your star is nothing but a star that no doubt views things as you do, and its flickering is nothing but fatigue at having to look in a way that has nothing to do with its feelings. Catita ... Catita, why does your destiny have to be in the sky? Your destiny is here on Earth, and I have it in my hands, and I feel a terrible urge to throw it over the railing into the sea. But no. What would you be without your destiny? Your destiny perhaps is to be a puddle on an ocean beach, a puddle full of seawater, but a puddle in which there is, instead of a paper boat, a little fish that raises a fat and brutish wave.

SERGIO ... HE HAD A NAME THAT DID NOT SUIT HIM ... a serene and chaste name, with a touch of the steppe, of fatality and of popishness. He was a boy with piggish eyes who sometimes, while he was up to some mischief, shot out apelike stares—small, sharp, and black. All of him was in his skin: such coldness, such nuance, such smoothness, and an amber light. He was also in his head: a crown of ribbons of curly, chestnut hair over a smooth forehead. I can remember him only as a name that passes quickly through a crowded, squat, fenced-off street, hiding his face in his hurry. He was also in the sound of his heels as he walked, the colorless dry sound of beaten wood. Sergio was in his whole figure. It was impossible to know anything else about him: nobody lied like Sergio, with his entire soul, beyond any truth or likelihood, far beyond .... And so it was, always. One day, Sergio became a priest. And nothing was ever heard from him again. Eugenio d'Ors, the distinguished Dominican philosopher, can write his life story—Sergio's or his own—with the sacred hope of finding out for certain why a boy with the eyes of a pig who lied like nobody else became a priest. And d'Ors could even recount his death to us in advance—Sergio's— under a crucifix as large and cruel as death itself, hanging from a word as simple as solitude, and a whole morning spent in his treacherous cell. And he could add great subtleties to the simplicity of the death of a priest with a scraggly beard that had once been young and highly sexual. Oh, what a marvelous book Eugenio d'Ors could write about Sergio's life and death! How fitting for a stupid and unmotivated life is the philosophy—so down to earth, so handsome, so nurturing, so charming, so ingenuous, so damn Catalonian—of this annotator! I seem to be reading: " … and so … But let us examine, Annotator, and may we not be carried away by love …. Measure … Compare …" But, I don't know why, once in a while I think that Sergio never died; that, at the hour of his death, he pretended to be dead; that he let himself be buried and then dug himself up two days later and returned to Lima to escape from the monastery and begin a new life. If only this were so … But then Eugenio d'Ors's book could not be written, and I would never learn anything about Sergio.

HE GRABBED ONE OF HER HANDS. SHE INSERTED ONE of her fat legs, either one, perhaps someone else's, under his right leg, which was bent back as if ready to kick. His face burned red like a traffic light or the sign for a late-night pharmacy. Suddenly it turned, and there appeared another face, identical to the first, only yellow. This was the sign to stop. She remained impassive like a prostitute. She smiled candidly, dug her leg in further, and bit her lower lip without blinking. Ramón grew thinner. She grew fatter. Ramón was a beast that was beginning to have ideas. She was a woman who was beginning to become a beast. Suddenly the sun lit up with a terrible, rose-colored light of alarm. The night train passed with a deafening roar. She and Ramón boarded the last car. A sad and dark freight car.

SHE WAS A FIERCE TASTER OF BOYS. ALL OF US WERE
to roll our heads over her firm, round little bosom. In this way,
from this inevitable love, we created an era: "When I wooed
Catita …" But it was Catita who wooed us. When we looked at
her, she winked without noticing. Her eyes: round like the rest
of her … And her name did not name her well. The *i* in the pen-
ultimate syllable made her long, dreary, distant: she who was
close, round, happy. And, above all, a sucker for love. Catalina
is a Gothic name; it makes one think of gray ogives at twilight,
of bronze moss-covered fountains, of dwarfed chaotic villages,
of bulky chastity belts … And Catita was a blond window at
noon; a clean, modern, white cement fountain; a large, tattered
sunshade for the beach; a schoolgirl's crazy hair ribbon … Lalá,
that's her real name. But Lalá was a quick and cautious girl. Lalá,
Lalá, Lalá … Soft heart and doll eyes and a laughing face. Ramón
threw himself into Catita like a swimmer into the sea, from head
to foot, hands first, then the head, and finally the feet: flexed and
worn down at the heels. Atop the staff of the month of Janu-
ary—still greased with dirty, cold clouds—Ramón hung in the
sky: in the air, in the middle, in balance, in his bathing suit, at
the very top, with a hundred trembling boys pushing him from

behind, onto Catita, the sea. Ramón had a bad fall—a belly flop that splashed all of us unprepared observers. Catita, a sea to bathe in at twelve o'clock noon with the stupefying sun overhead, a dry butterfly, jaundiced brambles, or a yellow bathing cap. Catita, a sea with waves because there are no old ladies, because there are boys … Catita, round sea surrounded by a semicircular pier, emblazoned with cities … Catita, subtle boundary between the high and the low tides … Catita, sea submissive to the moon and the bathers … Catita, sea with lights, seashells, with little potbellied boats, sea, sea, sea … O love without old ladies, straw sunshades, advice, genuflections … Catita, love, with fat and gentle hope, love that rises and falls with the moon, round love, close love, love in which to sink oneself, to snorkel about in with open eyes, love, love, love … Catita, sea of love, love of sea. Catita, anything and nothing … Catita—appearing in all the vowels, whole, complete, in body and soul, in the *a* and disappearing little by little, feature by feature, in the others; in the *e*: tender and foolish; in the *i*: skinny and ugly; in the *o*: almost her, but not quite … Catita is honest and pretty; in the *u*: albinistic and moronic. Catita, like some consonants, so much like the *b*, in her hands; the *n*, in her eyes; the *r*, in her walk; the *ñ*, in her personality; the *k*, in her character; the *s*, in her bad memory; and the *z*, in her good faith … Catita, a round field in the sea, a round kiss in love … Catita, sound, symbol … Catita, any old thing and exactly the opposite … Catita, in the end, as pretty, sincere, alive, and flirtatious as only she could be … To trap her was as impossible as stopping up with the tip of the index linger the flow of water from the mouth of a large spigot; flesh firm under the pressure of a touch, flesh that escaped through the cracks in the nail, through the lines on the skin; that jumped out at us; that, if deposited in a receptacle, quietly, would be only dense light, water to drink and to launch paper boats in. Water, water, water … And, in the end, a pretty, lovesick girl, a taster of boys, Catita …

ON THE ROOFTOP, THE UNIQUE AND MULTIPLE AIR, wrapped entirely around itself, rolling invisibly in currents like Bulgarian milk in bacillus culture; on the rooftop, in the air, dense with rubber bands made of sun, with colorless mucilage of humidity—on the rooftop—the wife's undergarments. It is here in the humid regions of the air where the blue of the sky is bluer, and when an unnamable bird goes past, it grows and grows as if seen through a magnifying glass. It is a window in the house's single story—a dreamy view into the gaping, dirty, insane room through glass whitened by the afternoon's oblique reflection, the gentleman's jacket with its silver chain and its watch hidden in the pocket. Through the same window appear—instead of the gentleman's flesh supported by the gentleman's clavicle—two naked spheres on top of the back of the Viennese chair. Old bones, already the appalling color of skeletons exhumed long years after burial ... With my back to the sun, I open with the shadow of my head a calyciform hole in the light of the glass. There they are, without the horror of a nightmare, the jacket and the chair—human, familiar, spontaneous, frank, at home. A pot-bellied gentleman. His cashmere jacket sags at the bottom and jokingly nags the wicker to fatten up, set it straight, fill it out ... The wicker: skinny, pious, a spinster. All the buttons on the jacket are closed except the last one whose corresponding buttonhole has the round and empty malice of an old man's eye; a truthful, sexual eye, out in the air like the lady's undergarments on the rooftop ... The jacket might be a sixty-year-old drunkard, a cynic, a womanizer, an oaf—if it had a nose, it would be red, oily, hairy, covered with pimples. In a silence that sounds abrupt, sudden, violent, we might believe we hear the ticktock of the clock, the jacket's impious and stubborn heart. The chain is arched and expresses nothing—hence, nearly horizontal, relaxed, it is the jacket's conscience. The wicker sits in the wooden chair with the most austere decency, as if she were in church or at a conference on domestic hygiene; the torso and thighs at right angles. She has eliminated her belly, her breasts, her legs, out of a sense of modesty; her arms, we know not why; her face, for the sake of decency. She has avoided sinning by removing one dimension from herself. That is why we imagine the wicker—two ascetic, round lividnesses—with a curl of hair on her forehead to banish bad thoughts; with only one gray hair in her black lacquer bun to remind her of death when she looks at herself in the mirror; with a mole on the tip of her nose, we don't know why; with a short Latin prayer on her lips to avoid useless words. The day cackles. A hen cackles like the day—secretive, implacable, manifest, discontinuous, vast. A frond rubs against a house as the chaste swallows protest. Above, the cirrus sky. Below is the street, extensively, energetically stained with light and shadow as if with soot and chalk. The gentleman's jacket belches, swells, and belches again. With their brooms, sharp and straight like paintbrushes, the street sweepers make drawings along the tree-lined streets. The street sweepers have the hair of aesthetes, the eyes of drug addicts, the silence of literary men. There are no penumbras. Yes, there is one penumbra: a burst of light in vain spreads through the street that grows longer and longer in order to cancel it out. Here a shadow is not the negation of the light. Here a shadow is ink: it covers things with an imperceptible dimension of thickness; it dyes. The light is a white floury dust that the wind disperses and carries far away. A shabby young girl inserts a cord into bare spools of thread. I insert wooden adjectives into the thick, rugged rope of an idea. At the end of the street, blocking it, a blue wall grows pale until it turns into the sky itself. This city is definitely not a village. The donkeys devoutly respect the sidewalks. Donkeys that only bray in the neighborhood at determined hours … Donkeys that do the unmentionable behind a tree or a pole without lifting a leg … Donkeys that dare not graze on the grassy patches but stick close to the cement edge of the gutters … Donkeys that sing like the roosters when the roosters oversleep … Donkeys on the side of the street with a sidewalk that graze on the low, cart-driver-beheading branches of the trees … Oh, these donkeys—the only remaining villagers in the city—have become municipalized, bureaucratized, humanized …! Donkeys want to be deemed worthy of obtaining their election rights: to elect and be elected … Through the kitchen odors of frying oil, a world enclosed within this world is revealed to me: the world of the barnyard. The roosters also become human, though not in a sane, patriotic, sensible way like the donkeys but rather in a strange, impertinent, exotic way. Not turning into men, but rather into Englishmen. As for the roosters: eccentric gringos who wear Scottish wool, engage in a foolish sport like worm-hunting, play golf with gnawed bones and cobs of corn, constantly shiver from the cold, rise at dawn, and do not understand females. Soon they will smoke pipes, read magazines, play polo—instant gentlemen—and take pleasure trips to Southampton on a P.S.N.C. ship. Hens are good mothers who still make an effort to please their husbands. Moral standards in the barnyard are falling. If it weren't for the solid good faith and austere habits of the ducks … If it weren't for the antimilitaristic and clerical traditionalism of the turkeys—scanty hygiene, bad smells, omissions, lawsuits, bad moods, great-great-grandfathers who were counts, mortgages … Female ducks don't know about the following things: the husband, the shop, themselves, the house, and the children; one must be eat well, be virtuous, and save for old age.

The ducks would disapprove of Nansen's trip to the South Pole. Ducks—I don't know why—always seem to be fighting with some aunt over a cursed inheritance. We don't know if the ducks descend from immigrants from the South or from some imaginary French consul, married to a Paraguayan woman and settled in Lima, where he died in 1832 or 1905. Rabbits have long ears, as we all know, but they are good fellows. Very little is known about them; they are, it is true, always well dressed, but they live in caves. One additional fact: they read Pitigrilli. We might say they are middle-class, meddlesome busybodies, know-it-alls with bastards in their family history … Soon they will acquire a late-model Ford limousine and a second-hand pianola. The girls are lovely. There will be weekly receptions. Where does the money come from? From nothing honorable, undoubtedly. Their fortune was gotten in a bad way, according to *vox populi*. The rabbits' friendship is very sought after by everyone. But if the rabbits are not decent people, absolutely decent, friendships will be revoked. Rabbits wink their alcoholic eyes, reddish in the sun, and hide their Semitic mouths. The geese are wealthy country gentlemen, always just passing through. They have a suspicious look in their eyes; their accent is from the mountains; their bellies are full; their families are back at the hacienda ... They never give alms. He and she ... Exemplary spouses. Both of them obese. Sometimes a goat—bad head, bad head, bad head ... he staggers like a sleepwalker. He is photophobic, like a good nocturnal bird. His age? ... Doesn't have one. Twenty years old ... Fifty years old ... These madcaps don't have an age, but rather a character; not a personality, but rather a vice ... or many vices. A face between that of Mephistopheles and Uncle Sam. He could have had a job in the government, but he doesn't, that devil of a goat. He is a cuckold without even having been married. He spouts bitter philosophies about matrimony. There is nothing as wonderful as having no commitments. Long live idleness, the good life! The goat gets bored; the goat gets bored; the goat gets bored ... Guinea pigs, all of them, male and female, are female. They are the servants of the turkey and the turkey hen. Their faces are small and swarthy; their eyes are small and shiny; they are short and bent; their step is small and lively. They are all that remain of the colonial warehouse Castile dismantled. The young turkeys call them "mommies." The horses prepare the traditional local dishes; they have suckled from the turkey mother, blown the turkey father's nose, they know all the family secrets, are disdainful of the ducks, and they never go out because they don't have enough money to buy new capes. They look like little old ladies: spouting proverbs—devout, ill-tempered gossipmongers. The pigeons are the scandal of the barnyard. The pigeons speak French, are indecorously sentimental, go everywhere alone, and are more than a little coquettish. Their Yankee partiality for couplets make them abstain when they get to the tenth floor, prompting the male pigeons to dress all in white and neglect their children.

The countryside—bloody with green blood. The cheeks and lips of some of the whimsical figurines are also green. The field's fat face has one gray eye of a puddle that laughs like an idiot. The other eye—the right one—is the sun, in the flesh and without a pupil. This landscape has spent five months in a mental hospital jumping up and down on one foot and tearing itself to pieces with ten black clawed fingers. This hysterical, masochist landscape with a history of syphilis ... This battered, rugged landscape ... This one-eyed and sexless landscape ... On its bare belly, the bruises from tilling. On its gray forehead, the boils of a clearing. On its chest, like a scapular, a strange fetish, the obsession of the church. The rain quiets the crazed landscape. Its visions are now tame, sane, almost true—the black, bovine afternoon is beaten on its opaque flanks, its rough haunches, with the heavy tail of the sun's rays: straight, yellow. And a cow, more real than anything, behind a mud wall, weaves moos through the tattered grass.

I DREAM OF AN ICONOGRAPHY OF RAMÓN THAT would allow me to remember him, so plastic, so spatial, plastically, spatially. All that remains for me of Ramón is the serious bitterness of having known him and his permission to leaf through his intimate diary in Miss Muler's silly little alcove; a trail of cigarette butts along the city's longest street and a way of thinking and seeing that makes it possible for me to live in the midst of this amorphous collection of houses, these un-caustic streets, these naive trees, this somewhat pesky, somewhat lagunalike sea, on this plane that suddenly acquires three dimensions and ten thousand inhabitants. Oh, the sea! Only the sea has not ceased to be, those long black waves, pencil lines meticulously equidistant from the thousands of curves along the beach. The sierra cannot be seen from the side, only from above, the high mountains in contoured lines; the hills hewn with an axe. The obsessive precision of canvases and projections, scales and numbers. May God bless Ramón, that madman who taught me to see the water in the sea, the leaves on the trees, the houses on the streets, the sex of women. Around here Ramón has become lines, lights, secrets, faces, ornaments, details, blades of grass, the ringing of bells ... No, no. An iconography, an album in black and sepia through whose pages he would pass, with his melancholy mouth, his illusory glasses, and his terrible insignificance, on his way anywhere. Or standing in front of rusty old sheds, or under green streetlights, or against yellow twilights. Or judiciously sitting at a parochial school desk or on the drunken benches along the esplanade, or on the slippery chairs of the electric streetcar. Or chasing girls (made of gelatin and organdy), or fat shadows, or lit windows, or unsociable dogs. With one leg outstretched or with both legs pressed tightly together. Inapprehensible, but indubitable, unmistakable. On difficult afternoons of light and tedium, I might open the album and ask Ramón: "What should I do now, my friend?" And he might answer as he used to during the happy days of his life in the sierra: "Whatever you want." And I would do what I wanted: walk through the streets that smell, at that hour, of honey and kitchen mops. Under the convex sky, a lemon peel turned inside out, sounds grow until they become visible, the trees sharpen their branches like cypresses, and an old man walking by pounding the cobblestones with his iron cane drags his shapeless shadow along the ground like a cloak. An automobile drives past at fifty miles per hour—a speed definitely prohibited—through a street traversed only by donkeys loaded with sandbags. The mayor is by now merely that gentleman with a pointed beard whom everyone should obey. Yesterday, the sun rose ten minutes after it should have risen. Something else: it penetrated the only place it should not have penetrated: between the ears of the only baker's ass we have left in the city. The cold has long white muscles like one of those emaciated athletes who sometimes carry off the trophy at a championship game, runts three feet tall and with the hands of a typist. The air rubs against the sky and scratches it the way a diamond scratches glass. I do whatever I want. A dove has carried away my last good thought. Now I am as I truly am: clean, Asiatic, refined, bad. Now I have a round rubber neck. Now I jump over an old woman on the street who stops to examine her shoe, poor old blind woman. Ramón loved the cooks who gave themselves to their bosses' sons in the barnyard, in the haystacks and brick piles where the birds brood. The bells of Saint Francis hum a light melody—the prior doesn't hear them. A section of the sky collapses over a cornet of the sea, on this side of the island. A closed, double window—the gesture of a decent house, the wink of a pharmacist's spectacles. In it will appear at night when nothing can be seen, a face that is pretty, pretty, pretty …

THE PAVING STONES — UNDERGOING NOONTIME heliotherapy, recumbent, facing the sun. In the corridor of the street—the windows of air have been opened—the policeman is the doctor who observes, who observes ... Among the paving stones there is only one clinically interesting case—a triangular stone on the corner, at the intersection of two sidewalks (Miss CV, twenty-three years old, daughter of consumptive parents. Miss CV swallows. Miss CV has her eyes closed. Miss CV dies. Uterine cancer? ... The name of the disease is unknown. Miss CV is a very interesting case.) The rest of the stones have -algias, -itis, -osis, all horribly general—married or widowed women who, in order to prolong the hour, prolong their convalescence. When it is impossible to have a lover because you are sixty years old, the best thing to do is to lie in the sun with your eyes closed and forget your husband, dead or alive. These sexual hours of dinner and digestion ... A good time of day at the sanatoriums. The one across the street in the shade is a row of sick individuals of the male sex, the allusive and tragic male sex. In their heads, dark and painful, pounds the fever of business. Through their veins and arteries, wagon carts come and go. In their ears, shrieks the chimes of the telephone. The smell of sickness, the smell of the taste of bile, become the smells of the office—the smell of cedar and reams of paper. A turkey buzzard, with its bent, sallow fortitude of a diabetic Norwegian, leaves for a station in the highlands of the Swiss sky, which has already turned on its ices, its snows, its hotels for the tourists ... the management of an oil company, fifteen years of equatorial, Venezuelan, xenophobic sunshine ... Bible readings, silent black beer, Swedish exercise, prodigiously not adjusting; the frugal, austere pleasures of a preseptentrional immigrant to this America—luminous, caliginous, brutish, hard, mineral, Miocenic, maritime ... The paving stones are stones carved with a hammer. The sun is killing them, but they do not complain. I don't know why they are here, suffering without being paid. Twenty little tailless mongrel dogs (large ears; the hanging ones are of sheepskin, the erect ones of felt) that range in color from the waxen hue of fresh straw to the bluing on steel, rush along behind one large purebred dog with a tail and a mundane, uncouth, opulent face ... The dogs glide along on short, agile limbs. The sun turns all the dogs into gold ingots. Hungering after the great female ... The social revolution ... Princess Alexandra Canoff, running down this street—almost as solitary and sunny as Tsarskoye Selo—your Parisian follies are now over. Freud does not include Caron's or Cory's perfumes among his coprolitic smells ... This bitch smells like *The Night before Christmas*, like *A Night in Siam*, like I don't know what night, just so long as it's not an afternoon. What a good idea it is to give the names of nights to perfumes. All perfumes are nocturnal. Sometimes I think that flowers exist only to temper the emotions of the day. In the desert, the very same sun that is merely a jovial and idle Barranco sun shining on these rose gardens becomes Libyan, Saharan; this matchmaking sun without a family is a bachelor, a gossipmonger from all five continents; a bluffer; this gallant sun that offers his arm to forsaken aunties on esplanades ... Flowers absorb light and heat and carbon gas in the process. At night, wherever there is a flower, there is also a gnomic light with a tender halo of heat enclosed within the coquettish shade of each corolla. The sea is also the outskirts of the city. Now the sea is a mirror that reflects the sky, a thick and enormous looking glass quicksilvered with mullets and corbinas. The sea is green because the sky is green. The sky, an immense face, green and featureless ... The sea can be a picturesque, naive sea full of fish. But now it is a mirror. The sky can be a field for farming or livestock. But it isn't; now it is a face that looks at itself in the mirror of the sea. A heartsick lamp in a street that could have been and wasn't ... ; in the land breeze, the stump of a sidewalk, and that spirit of foolish desire common to all streets. A rooster turns to me with a cruel, mechanical gesture, its bald head, its sharp ivory profile, its carmine British ears. The sea hoists tar-covered birds and bundles of waves with the crane of the rusty island. The opaque marine solarium— sunlight rusted by water—trickles of oil at any given moment, suddenly, a large splash of mercury that flounders, that sinks ... A mine from the Great War, a broken egg from Moirae ... I don't know which inadvertent slope in the streets always takes me to the outskirts of town. The sea is the outskirts as well.

THE AFTERNOON ARISES FROM THIS SLOW-MOVING, dapple-gray mule with a long stride. It emanates from her in waves that make visible the light of three o'clock postmeridian and reveal the canvas of the atmosphere, a movie screen—but a round one that does not need shadows; all things emanate from her. At the end of each sheaf of rays: a house, a tree, a lamp, myself. This mule is creating us as she imagines us. Through her I feel the solidarity of my origins with the animate and the inanimate. We are all images conceived during a calm and supple trot, images that become foliated, plastered, and fenestrated, or dressed in drill, or topped with a glass helmet. Cosmic logic divides us up into undefined species of only one kind ... window and I ... sea gull and I ... With each step the mule takes—a step that is duplicate, rotund, eternally inalterable, predetermined by a divine genius—my being trembles at unknowable destiny. At this moment the mule has never existed. The mule has been cancelled as she turns a corner. Now the afternoon is itself—atheistic, autogenetic, romantic, liberal, desolate. These famished dogs—mute scavengers with protruding backbones, sagging hides, and arched bodies—look like cats, street cats with realistic, socialistic, enlightened, herbivorous eyes. A gust

109

of wind unfurls a Chinese flag at a towering height, as if it were a parchment, from left to right—the flag veils precisely that rectangle of the sky where the sun is. The afternoon grows black, and it becomes night. The poles, along these streets of low and nitrous walls, have the rather violent appearance of pedestrians. The day, with its invariably rainy mood, holds them for its fourteen hours at the edge of the sidewalk. Soon after nightfall, the poles begin to walk. Summer nights poured like black beer with gray, star-studded foam ... The poles were working very hard, they grew tired, were widowed, their only son went to Guatemala ... By now their arms are falling off from just plain old age. And if their backs are not bent, it is only because their bones are made of wood. Aged electricians with hands dried and corroded by the gutta-percha and balata gum, by leaking batteries, and greasy tools ... They are retired and have acquired, along with the pleasure of a full pension and the right to frolic, the lines of certain former public officials who have fallen out of favor with the present government, survivors of distant battles, eccentric old uncles who gather herbs and collect postage stamps ... Between one pole and the next there is a distance of eighty feet that never decreases or increases—the poles neither love nor hate one another ... misanthropy, misogyny, at the most a grumble of irritation or a greeting from one to the other, and this only because they can't not do so ... At night the poles go for walks. On a street quite far away, I recognized a pole that spends the whole day at the door of my house with hat in hand, stiff and thoughtful, as if suffering quietly from a pain in the kidneys or doing arithmetic in its head. The poles never gather. During these strange walks the distances between them remain constant; they tie ropes around their waists: mountain climbers on the mountain of their lives at twenty-five degrees below zero. We attribute to them the reckless daring of men without families or trite pleasures—a Count Godeneau-Platana, pederast and Egyptologist; another Prince Giustati, Castilian and aesthete; a Mexican millionaire suddenly impoverished by a revolution ... The following morning (mornings always follow) the poles return to their assigned places. And there they are while fourteen gyrating hours mutate the color of the air—long, skinny, erect, rigid, wondering whether or not it will rain. One pole is called Julián, because he lets his beard grow ... the beard: paper streamers from the carnival of 1912. Another pole is called Matías, because that is his name. A poor asthmatic pole on Mott Street dreams of buying an overcoat made of French fabric. There are poles that cater to dogs. There are poles that are friends of beggars. There are European poles with the green eyes of crystal insulators. There are streetlight poles. There are telephone poles.

AN ICE CREAM VENDOR'S TRUMPET DREW ATTENTION to a nocturnal howling of dogs, symphony of tin and moon, rip-roaring from the beginning, a rip that exposed black, canine palates bristling with taste buds as hard as calluses. If their singing could be musically annotated, it would have to be done on a temperature scale, on graph paper, with a dotted line, with odd numbers. Musical skeleton. Forty-two degrees Fahrenheit: a fatal fever. A whirlwind of light and dust rises to the sun from a nearby field surrounded by thick adobe walls. A contemptible soaring wind that lifts the whirlwind, catching it without bending it. Hidden, childish, imprisoned air . . . Above the mud entablature, and behind it, is an evil comet, the upper funnel broken along the wind's axis; the tilt of an elliptic circumference; a clear, closed curve. At night this street will be a different street. We shall walk by here without knowing where we are going. At noon, footsteps make no sound. The shadow follows alongside—dwarfed, shapeless, the silhouette of an unkempt gangster feigning an attack. Silence closes its parentheses in each window. Ramón, shaving soap, green blanket, holy palm at the head of his bed—and at the window, barely opened onto the heat of a yellow sky; oh, second floors in a low town!—an oozing eucalyptus tree that drops round moments into the painted gutter, delicate balls of scorched paper, burned and rolled-up leaves—folk medicines, ancient recipes, rest, rest … Sweaty, dark-skinned girl, suddenly so ugly with a mere gesture, so pretty if you stand under the light at the edge of the pavement, breath of summer, afternoon nap dreams … You make my steps fall into rhythm with yours. I don't know what to say to you. A sudden gust of cold wind changes our lives. You disappear from my consciousness at every instant, and when you reappear, you are warm, like the hat or the book we leave in the bright sun when we escape to the shade. The wide street opens our eyes, violently, until it hurts and blinds us. The whole town drags itself along … poles, trees, people, streets … along the banks of this stream of freshness and sea breezes. In the oven of summer, the houses made of bread dough bake and get burned on the bottom. You no longer walk by my side. A sexton extinguished the sun with a willow branch. And six steel bells—*Ite missa est*—ritualistic, mechanical—spoke simply. The sultriness is over, as is our sitting still, the tedium of being indoors, and the inevitable shadow of this four-hour mass.

A Previously Omitted Fragment

The following fragment, omitted from the book when published, appeared as an extract in the magazine Amauta, *no. 10, Lima, December 1927.*

WHAT WERE OUR IDEAS? THE TRUTH WAS, WE DIDN'T have any. We believed vaguely in very vague vaguenesses. Ramón doubted everything. I had screaming dreams about the monarchy. A mad and sainted king, a Phillip the Second who would make me his prime minister ... I would send Ramón to Peking as a special ambassador, and I would build a castle out of glazed tiles on the peak of San Cristóbal ... I would give food to everybody, and I would turn anybody who complained into my favorite ... Ramón believed that feeding imbeciles was an imbecility, but he believed that grudgingly. Lucho Mos was terribly socialistic; he carried around in his wallet a greenish caricature of Marx and a list of people to execute; he didn't go to Mass on Sundays or other holy days, but he did take communion at Lent. Manuel was the absurd mentor of those absurd boys: in response to a distinguished quote from one of us, he would punctually repeat in cursive the famous reply of So-and-so in such-and-such a chapter of such-and-such a book. Manuel believed everything at the moment he said it, and he was, therefore, the one most sure of his own words, which belonged to others but were magnificent.

Afterword

This poem was written in response to a letter to Adán from Celia Paschero, an associate of Jorge Luis Borges, who was coming to Lima to do research for her doctoral thesis, Contemporary Peruvian Poetry. *The letter read:*

The reason for this letter? Apart from wanting to express my affection for you, I have another goal: to request information about your life, information told, if possible, with all the spice you know how to sprinkle on everything you say and write. I have proposed writing an article about you for *La Nacion* ... I have just started publishing with them, and I want to write one that is human, through which your blood and skin can be felt ... I know this whole business might be loathsome to you. But in the name of the warmth there has been between us since the first moment we met, of the affection I feel and of my profound admiration for you, please agree to my request. Leave aside all your bohemianism and pour it all out to me and ... speak to me about yourself. Can you?

Written Blindly

You want to know about my life?
I know only of my footsteps,
of my weight,
of my sadness
and my shoe.
Why ask who I am, where I'm going?
Because you know plenty about the Poet, the harsh
and sensitive volume of my human self,
which is my body and vocation,
nonetheless.

If I was born,
the Year remembers my birth,
but I don't remember,
because I live, because I kill myself.

My Angel isn't a Guardian Angel,
my Angel is of Satiety
and Remnants,

and carries me endlessly,
stumbling, always stumbling
in this dazzling shadow
that is Life
and its deceit
and its charm.

When you know everything …
When you know not to ask …
but to chew instead
on your mortal fingernail,
then I will tell you my life,
which is no more than one more word …

The whole of your life is like each wave:
knowing how to kill,
knowing how to die,
and not knowing how to tame plentitude,
and not knowing how to wander and then return to the source,
and not knowing how to hold longing …

If you want to know about my life
go look at the Sea.
Why do you ask me, Learned One?
Don't you know that in the World,
everything gathers from nothing,
from withering immensities,
nothing but an eternal trace
barely a shadow of desire?

The real task, if that's what you'd take on,
is not to understand life but to imagine it.
The real isn't captured: it is followed,
and that's what dreams and words are for.
Beware its shortcuts ...
Beware its distances ...
Beware its crags ...
Beware its herds ...

Who am I?
I am what I am,
ineffable and innumerable,
the figure and soul of rage.
No, that was at the end ... and at the beginning
before the beginning began.
I am a body of subdued fury
and sullen irony.
No, I am not one who seeks the poem,
not even life ...
I am an animal hunted by its own being,
which is a truth and a lie.

My being is so simple, and so choked,
a sting of nerves and flesh ...

I was looking for another,
and that's been my search for myself,
I've never wanted, and don't want now, to be me,
but rather another who was saved
or who will be,

not one of Instinct, who gets lost,
or of Understanding, who retreats.

My day is a different day,
some days I don't know where to put myself,
I don't know where to go in my jungle
among my reptiles and my trees,
my books and mortar
and neon stars
and women who close around me like a wall,
    or like no one … or like a mother,
and the newborn who cries over me
and through the streets,
all the wheels, primal and real.
Such is the whole of my days,
till my last afternoon.

The Other, that Neighbor, is a ghost.
Is there air you breathe that chokes you
and recreates you,
breathing your inane body?
No! Nothing is more than the endless surprise
of finding yourself again,
always you, the same you, between the same walls
of distances and streets …
And of skies, those roofs
that never kill me because they never collapse!

I never gain the fury of the divine
or the sympathy of the human.

I'm this way without regret.
That's not how I feel.
By day I am the Loner,
and the Absolute of Zoology, if I think about it,
or like a ferocious carnivore, if I take hold.
Am I the Creature or the Creator?
Am I Matter or Miracle?
Your question is so much mine, so alien … Who am I?
Do you think I know?
But no, the Other doesn't exist,
only I, in my terror and orgasm!

With all my dreamed-again dreams
and all the coins collected
and all my body
resurrected after every coitus,
blind, futile, eyeless …

When you're no more than being
and if you reach the age of dying
and when you truly know
where life and death cross …
Then I will tell you who I am,
certainly, and without a voice, my friend!

The pure animals who speak to you
heal themselves with potent herbs,
there, among immaterial stones …
the world of the real, and human sciences,
where supposed foul-smelling boys

have had fun with a ball.
Yes, life is delirium …
and yet my nothingness
never was in this life, none of it …
but real, but blue
or volcanic.

How late Time comes to the moment of forgetting
and prudence.
It comes dragging along,
like a flood of clouds and earth and the human.

How one comes to oneself at the wrong time!
How unforeseen and desperate is every now,
every *I* that collapses with Time,
never always and always never.
Eternal unsleeping dawn
in which I resolve myself to my deeds
and my thinking!

Loneliness is a hard rock
against which the Air is hurled,
it's in every wall of the City,
complicit and hiding.
I hurl myself again and again, ceaselessly,
I am my hazard, my creating.

Poetry, my friend,
is inexhaustible, incorrigible, indwelling.

It is the infinite river,
all blood, all meandering, all ruin,
dragging along what we live …
What is the Word
but a vain and varied shout?
What is the image of the Poetic
but a log moving quickly beneath the nullity of a cat?
It's all a flood
and if it weren't
nothing would be real …
nothing the same.

Love knew only
to swallow its substance.
This is how Creation renewed itself.
For me, all was yesterday, but I'm alive,
and sometimes I believe,
and the moment suckles me

I'm not one who knows.
I'm the one who no longer believes,
not in man,
not in woman,
not in a single story house,
not in a pancake with honey.
I'm no more than a word
flying out of my forehead
taking pity on itself and maybe nesting
somewhere high above this sad spring.

As for Being,
don't ask me again,
I no longer know …

And I knew simply that I was no longer
what I was not,
I don't know how,
and that everything was part of my nothingness.
And I was,
I don't know when,
chasing between the numinous and the mire,
inside it all,
I, born, scrawny, already fully armed,
and with every step I took
chasing it … the word,
any word,
one from a burrow
or the one that leaps.

If my life isn't this
what could life be?
A puzzle?
May time, besides its own, give me Time,
and I will remake my eternity,
which is no longer mine
because I discarded it …
It was mine for one moment too long …

Have you heard of the abandoned ports
of lunacy and departure,

of the cetacean with its drenched costume
that does not swim … and founders?
Have you known so much about the city
that rather than a city
it seems like a dismembered corpse,
myriad and infinitesimal?

You know nothing.
You know only to ask.
You know only wisdom.
But wisdom is not to be with no thought
of anything at all:
but rather to keep on,
on foot, into now.

TRANSLATED BY RICK LONDON AND KATHERINE SILVER